Zenzele

Zenzele

A LETTER FOR MY DAUGHTER

Nozipo Maraire

WEIDENFELD & NICOLSON

London

First published in Great Britain in 1996 by
Weidenfeld & Nicolson

The Orion Publishing Group Ltd
Orion House
5 Upper Saint Martin's Lane
London WC2H 9EA

A catalogue record for this book is available
from the British Library

ISBN 0 297 81626 8 [cased]
ISBN 0 297 81627 6 [paperback]

Typeset at The Spartan Press Ltd,
Lymington, Hants

Printed in Great Britain by
Clays Ltd, St Ives plc

This novel is dedicated to the memory of my father,
the late Dr Nkosana Arthur Maraire,
whose love, laughter and lore kindled my spirit
and gave me the courage to pursue my dreams.

TRIBUTE

There have been so many who have lightened the load of this long journey.

I am indebted to the Maraire clan for keeping the spirit of our ancestors alive and passing on our heritage through each generation. With love to Tete Mai Zano, whose open arms have engulfed our sorrows. I also thank my adopted families, John and Sue de Cuevas and Dr Kombo and Maria Moyana, not only for the peaceful retreats, the unwavering support, and sound counsel but, most importantly, for giving me back my sense of home. I have been inspired by women of sensitivity and courage, especially Dr Angelina Mbauya (my mother), Mrs Nozipo Maraire (my grandmother) and Dr Peggy Dulany (my tia-amiga and role model). I thank Dr Dennis Spencer, my clinical mentor, for his global vision, teaching and his humanity, and all of my colleagues in neurosurgery, for their dedication and companionship. I am particularly grateful to Dr Celia Chao for being a thoroughly biased critic. To Ameneh Ziai and Julie Kahn for sisterhood. To Mats Berdal for crossing the ocean. To the late Tiyane Chitepo for unsettling me with his love.

I am greatly indebted to Roslyn Targ, my ever-energetic agent, for believing in *Zenzele*, and to Elsbeth Lindner and Carol Taylor, my editors, for their patience.

Finally I reserve a special thanks for Joanne Washington Blodgett and Papa Madiaw Ndiaye, for the tenacity of their affection across so many continents and through so much tragedy. Thank you for always being there.

GLOSSARY OF TERMS

Aluta continua	The struggle continues
Amai	Mother
Amandla	Freedom
Baas	Form of address to European masters, similar to the word 'boss'
Baba	Father
Babamukuru	Grandfather or oldest uncle
Chakowa	A village in the eastern highlands in Manicaland
Derere	Okra
Great Zimbabwe	Ancient site of African civilization dating to 300 B.C.
Here hamuna we	Expression of amazement
Jira (*machira*, pl.)	Traditional cotton cloth, used as a wrap, scarf, mat, etc.
Kanjani	Hello, how are you?
Kopjes	Rocky hills
Kumusha	Rural homeland
Kwuame Nkrumah	First president of Ghana
Lobola	Bride price
Matikiti	Pumpkin
Matumbu	Intestines
Mauyu	A fruit
Mbuya and Ambuya	Grandmother
Mealie meal	Corn meal

Mjiba	Young woman revolutionary
Morowe	Hello
Mukoma	Used preceding the name of an older brother or cousin; alone means 'brother–sister'
Mwauya	Welcome
N'anga	Witch doctor
OAU	Organization of African Unity (a regional political forum for African leaders)
Pamberi ne chimurenga	Forward with the struggle (revolutionary slogan)
Robben Island	A grim jail for political prisoners
Sadza	Starch staple of Zimbabwe
Sekuru	Grandfather
Léopold Senghor	A cultural leader of Senegal and former head of state
Shiri	Bird
Sisi	Used preceding the name of an older sister or cousin; also commonly used for maid; alone means 'sister'
Ian Smith	Last white prime minister of Rhodesia. He vehemently opposed majority rule
Tete	Aunt (father's sister)
Tsika	Dignity and integrity
Umvumvumvu	A river in Chakowa
Va	A formal term. It has no English equivalent; can be translated often to 'of' (e.g. Baba va Zenzele – father of Zenzele)

There is no word for cousin in our language. Consequently, cousins call one another brother and sister, so in the text a younger cousin calls her older cousin Mukoma (if male) or Sisi (if female).

Zenzele,

Today is the first day of winter, I believe. There is a thin frost on the ground that makes the white wall almost silver and casts a pallor on the garden. Not a single bloom remains; they all shuddered and collapsed as the air grew cool. Even the shrubs and trees are curling back their leaves in retreat, huddling together and bending low, close to the earth, to seek refuge. There is a ghostly glow and a glacial stillness all around, outside and within. There is something mournful about a winter dawn. It is a time of death, of loss, of flight.

It is still early – not even Samuel is awake – and I am sitting in the kitchen, sipping my morning tea, looking out at the backyard. As my strength falters, I love to spend the early hours of the morning in the orange glow of the dawn that fills the kitchen. I look out at the garden, whose face changes in subtle and beautiful ways every day. I have a most privileged seat at the season's opening of nature's theatrics. But perhaps the real reason that I creep quietly down in the mornings is that here I am reminded of you. This was your stage and my refuge. It is here that we encountered each other. I have a vivid image of you on the day you announced your plans:

I

glowing brown skin that defies the indignities that you subject it to (chlorine pools, Chimanimani winds and Chakowa sun) and that lively tangle of black curls cropped short as you insisted. You, with restless confidence, expounding on the necessity of going abroad for university. For months you carried that bright-red prospectus like a new Bible. There was undeniable proof of the merits of an American college education. During my spring cleaning I was tempted (with fervent urging by your siblings) to discard it accidentally. We watched keenly as it grew more and more tattered from constant use. We patiently waited. It was simply a matter of time before it disintegrated and our sermons would cease. Until then, any heretic was immediately set aright by the printed word, the gospel truth of higher education, as proclaimed by that book. I became the unfortunate target of your crusade.

'Mama, they have so many subjects. Look, the psycho-analytic theories of political anthropology! I don't even know what that means. And twenty libraries, for *one* university. They even have museums, Mama, full of art and it's *on the campus*.' You gushed, already picking up the jargon.

'Look here, Mama, the professors are from all over the world. Here's one – Professor Dao Wong Ng from Vietnam and – look at this – Professor Miguel Rodrigues Carrera Maria de dos Santos from Argentina. I'll bet he thanks his parents for that! Just imagine, Mama. Oh, look, I could even learn Polish. Ha-ha. There is no limit, Mama, don't you see!'

You looking up at me, eyes wide and round like the globe you long to conquer. I heard no more. Your mind is set, I see. You are going to fly away and leave my nest.

'I am not going to war, Mama, don't look like that.' Softly now, taking my arm. 'It is only a four-year course.'

'I will call every week and every holiday I shall hop on the first plane headed for Harare. Promise.'

Ah. But I know better. There will be summer writing workshops, dancing classes and bicycle tours, there will be Paris and London waiting to be discovered by you. I begrudge you not one single joy of youth, especially you who have the energy to embrace life. I finally gave in. But all I could think was, America? Harvard? Thousands of miles from Harare. I took up my ironing board, leaving you dancing to your chant of opportunities. America – so far away.

Was I too distant? Perhaps. I was often bewildered by the task of motherhood, that precarious balance between total surrender and totalitarianism. How could I prepare you for a world that I did not even understand? I was struck by the absurdity of my predicament as a woman. I had been excluded from the social contract that drafted and perpetuated those very rules that it fell to my lot to inculcate into you. Had it been up to me, I would have constructed a very different world for you. There would have been more laughter, more colour, less struggle. But despite my reality, you have made your own world. Of all my children, you are the only one who has created yourself.

Mine was a simple life. As the eldest of five children, I had many chores to do, and one duty: to make mother's load easier. Together, we calculated school fees, allotted the household spending money, bought uniforms and stationery. We pooled our earnings, subtracted the food and rent, and hid the remainder in an earthen jar behind the maize sacks in the pantry. We saved for birthdays and

Sunday dresses. Ours was a close but practical relationship. We were allies in a battle against hunger and
squalor. I did not weep over the starving in Ethiopia, the
refugees in Mozambique, the students of Soweto, nor
did it ever occur to me to lend my fury to a march against
rape and sexual violence. I signed no appeals to poli-
ticians, I did not sit on cold pavements, with fingers
frozen and my toes numb, to denounce neocolonialist
foreign domination. I have watched in wonder as you did
all of these. In my day I yearned for little else than my
own room with pretty blue curtains and a bedspread to
match where I could sleep alone instead of listening to
my little sister Farai's snoring and suffer the bruises of
Linda's flailing limbs. I wanted only peace. I yearned to
escape from the world and its hardships. You mustn't
wonder, then, that I am startled when you burst into the
kitchen, demanding, 'Mother, what do you think of
global warming?' My mind flashes a picture of a beach in
Jamaica, then goes blank. I often feel compelled to
prepare for a conversation with you. But I could never
keep up. You weave so many subjects into one, then,
having thoroughly dissected one issue, you launch with
equal passion into another. I am not only defeated; I am
exhausted.

Nothing gives me greater pleasure, therefore, than to
sit with my knitting and watch you debating with your
father. I am reassured to see that even the internationally
renowned lawyer is vulnerable. I inwardly delight to see
him falter to keep pace with your sharp wits. I can see
you, on those evenings, your features distorted from the
consolidation of mental faculties and your eyes, merciless, ready to pounce on any minor flaw in his argument.

We have the same eyes, you and I. But yours are still
vulnerable. They are candid and honest; like a scrupulous

4

documentary, they take note of all the details of life. And all of the world is reflected there – the beautiful and wretched alike. My eyes are resigned to observe, detached, from some distance. They want no part; they do not take in. They keep out. In your company, I often feel blind, groping for firm objects, hesitant lest I collide with some obstacle I cannot characterize, let alone surmount. Ah. But your fingers are truly mine, long, dark and graceful. And those clumsy lips, those are mine too. They fall and tense and bend into every shape. They are never still, never without expression.

The world is full of so many more illustrious and better qualified women – bankers, lawyers, doctors and presidents – who would have served as far superior role models. But I alone had the responsibility of being your mother and so, by default, your guide and mentor. I have learned something in my awkward journey through womanhood. The lessons are few but enduring. So I hope that you will pardon this curious distillation of traditional African teaching, social commentary and maternal concern. These are the stories that have made me what I am today. It is just that you are my very own, and it is an old woman's privilege to impart her wisdom. It is all that I have to give to you, Zenzele.

II

I know that you dislike the heat of the village at Christmas. I can sense your resentment when, on bended knee, you must pass the basin of water to every member of our large clan, in strict cultural hierarchy, to wash their hands before each meal and special rite. But it is part and parcel of the other traditions that you adore, like the singing of hymns late at night, just before bed. With Mbuya's thin, high voice almost transparent in its clarity, cutting through the stillness of the Chakowa night. Then the resonance as the menfolk boom their basses in. One hymn evokes the memory of others. There is always someone's favourite. All that is needed is a nostalgic 'Remember the one we used to sing at school?' Or 'Can't you just see Babamukuru singing this one?' Or 'Who taught us that one, remember, Mbuya?' And then we all join in afresh. Only Mbuya has the authority to disband our chorus with her firm whisper: 'Shall we pray?' Giggling softly, heads bent low, lest Mbuya catch sight of your playful grins (her hearing failing now), you and your cousins, all jostling for a piece of soft, warm carpet, descend to bended knee. I love those prayers best of all. It is a time when each of us, from the eldest to little Joy, gives expression to what lies deep, what is not for others to ask but that which longs to be shared. Through our supplications, the world comes into Mbuya's front parlour those evenings. I have always felt that God's spirit dwells in Chakowa, far from civilization and deep in the African countryside, and that if by chance we dared to open our eyes, if we peeped through the lace curtains during those evening prayers, His warm, loving eyes would peer right back.

And then bed. It is difficult for you to share a bed with others, I know. But Mbuya's tumbling home was built for a family of six, not twenty! Three generations with their friends and guests quite overwhelm the old farm-house. Happily, the boys adore sleeping out on the veranda. They feel it is an adventure, a sure sign of manhood, to brave the elements with only the shower of stars above to shelter them. And Mbuya with her candle, wandering from one room to the next, like a sea captain on deck, chuckling and mumbling as she goes, leaving wet kisses indiscriminately on every cheek, your father's and Joy's alike, without regard to rank, profession or age, and with a sweeping glance making sure that all is in order. Satisfied that her crew is safe and accounted for, she rings for one last cup of tea, makes sure her chamber pot is stored at a convenient distance under her bed, and sleeps. All those memories, all the richness of our little traditions, are yours. You may accept or reject them, but they form your foundation. They are your very roots. In years to come you will be nurtured by them.

Even the 'ancients', as you call them, with their interminable, glorious epic tales of battles waged and won and village life before the white man came – they are our living history. The village is our library. You were raving about the twenty in Cambridge; think of the thousands in Chakowa! And those *mbuyas* and *sekurus* are our encyclopaedias. How could I allow you to grow up reading Greek Classics, Homer's *Iliad*, the voyages of Agamemnon, and watch you devour *The Merchant of Venice* and *Romeo and Juliet* yet be ignorant of the lyrical, the romantic and the tragic that have shaped us as Africans? It is for that reason alone that while your other friends are off to London on summer holidays, we load the cars and trek off to 'the end of the earth'.

And as soon as we arrive the 'ancients' descend upon the house. 'All they want is Baba's imported whiskey, Mama, they do not come to see us.' I remember how you used to flee at their approach. How you winced in the embrace of those tattered, often toothless villagers reeking of sweat and local beer. With a joyful cry, they would take those graceful, piano-and-tennis hands into their calloused, sowing-and-harvesting hands, squeezing them tight as they ask you in with their eyes. Sekuru Isaac has always been particularly fond of you. Whenever he saw you he never failed to exclaim.

'Ah! She grows ever more beautiful, Amai Zenzele. You shall have to give her to one of my sons soon. He-he. She shall be a daughter-in-law I can be proud of.' Once when you were thirteen, you actually ran off in tears of disgust and fury.

'Mama, how *could* you let him say that? You laughed; I heard you, Mama! How could that horrible old man say such things? I would rather die than marry one of his stupid, smelly sons!' It was difficult for me to explain then. Sekuru Isaac is a simple and honourable man, an old friend of your grandfather's. The old man had meant no harm. On the contrary: he meant to give you the greatest compliment he could.

The summer following that incident it took me two

8

full hours to convince you to return. Do you remember that evening upstairs in Joy's room, packing her clothes and playthings for the trip to Chakowa? It was boiling in Harare which meant that Chakowa would be scorching! You were particularly reluctant as you had had an invitation to spend part of the holiday with the Makororos, visiting Victoria Falls.

'Mama, the Makororos are originally from Chakowa too, yet Petranella never spends even a weekend there. Yesterday in class she said that she would rather die than spend her holiday toasting in the bush with no electricity or running water. Why do we have to?' you pleaded, folding Joy's little frocks into her bright-yellow bag.

I knew the family and many like them who have forsaken our roots, still regarding the countryside as the 'tribal trust lands' of colonial invention. They were something to put behind one. The rural areas were places one moved from: it was a sign of progress. Naturally, to go back was a regression. Our *kumushas* have lost their meaning. Instead of being our cultural reposits and homelands, they are where the forgotten live and the dead are buried. Even those who grew up there among the *kopjes*, the baobab trees and the Umvumvumvu River – those big businessmen and cabinet ministers with sleek, dark Mercedes, who once herded goats and cows thick in the thorny bush of the eastern highlands – have forsaken it for the concrete splendour of the gleaming high-rises of the big cities. They are now too comfortable in the air-conditioned office blocks in Harare, Bulawayo and Mutare to return here. It is no surprise, then, that the rural areas, like obsolete factories, appear dilapidated and neglected. They are in a state of social and economic decay. For every school there are ten beer halls. Each has a blaze of lights, a lively atmosphere, bursts of laughter, cool drinks to relieve the heat, clinking of glasses and the melodic beckoning of the scratchy gramophone blaring American rhythm and blues. Like those bright, fluorescent but lethal mosquito traps, they attract and suck the life of our people. It is precisely us, the urban corps, who must renovate our *kumushas*. But these sentiments, I knew, would hardly mitigate your disappointment and your dread of returning to Sekuru Isaac's gnarled arms. And it certainly did not explain why you had to come along. I must have seemed cruel that day for I was particularly adamant.

'We are going all together. Petranella is going to be with her family and you shall be with yours. End of discussion, Zenzele.'

I watched your lips expressing the disappointment your words could not. I bit mine too but I had good reason for withholding my permission. Two days earlier, at the Borrowdale Shopping Centre, I had bumped into Petranella's mother, Florence Makororo. She cornered me in the bakery section of the super-market. After chatting for a few minutes she burst out: 'Amai Zenzele, I don't know what to do. Somewhere, somehow we have done the wrong thing.'

'What is the matter, Amai Stephen?' (I can just see you wincing whenever I would use the traditional titles in greeting.) She looked genuinely in need of company so after depositing the shopping at home I dropped in at her house for tea. I had last seen her at her father-in-law's funeral two weeks earlier. I had rather thought she was handling things well. As I parked my car behind hers in the drive I wondered whatever could be the matter. From the outside, everything appeared so calm. The house was a beautiful English-cottage style. The gardener, who had opened the gate, returned to his pruning of the shrubs. He had quite a job, for the garden was magnificent and vast, having been sculpted and landscaped by Sir Eliot Stoddard especially for the Marquess of Dryden, who had lived there for forty years before fleeing the country in a panic at Independence, fearing a sudden anarchic Marxist overthrow. I had always adored the grounds here. I would ask Florence if my own gardener, Samuel, could come over and spend some time learning from hers.

She came to the door as soon as I knocked.

'Yes, Amai Zenzele. Thank you so much for coming over. It has been too long since we sat down and chatted,' she said half-apologetically, ushering me into the lounge. As we sat down, she shouted over her shoulder to a dark corridor that led off to the right. 'Petranella! Come and greet Auntie.'

It was several minutes before a reluctant Petranella emerged and extended her hand. She was always an attractive girl, tall and slim, but somehow ill at ease in her gaunt frame, so that she moved with awkward jerking motions. There was something about her that reminded one of a horse. Perhaps it was the way her face, punctuated by a wide, fleshy mouth, jutted out, or maybe the nervous restlessness of her feet, or possibly it was her distinctive mane of shiny plaited dreadlocks that gave the impression that at any moment she would fling her head back and, with a snort, gallop off.

'Why not get us some tea, Pettie?' I was surprised to hear her mother say this like a plea. Her daughter glared defiantly.

'I think Sisi Selina is in the kitchen. I shall have her make it for you.' Then she turned from the clouded face of her mother to enquire timidly of me, 'How is Zenzele, Auntie?'

'She is very well, thanks, my dear. I left her at home playing tennis with her brother and a friend. When are you going to come and visit us?'

'I . . . I don't know, Auntie.' She seemed quite flustered, and she darted off to the kitchen to instruct the maid, Selina, to give us tea. It is the norm in our culture that the eldest daughter of the household acts as a hostess, especially when close family friends visit. She was not actually expected to prepare anything, just coordinate and serve tea with grace. But Petranella had made her point quite clearly. Tea-making was the maid's job – she had more important things to do. In our culture this was singularly rude of her and I knew that her mother was embarrassed.

'My, these girls grow up fast! It seems just yesterday that they were at crèche – do you remember those orange aprons they had to wear?' I said, meaning to be cheerful. But my comments did not evoke a happy reflection, only a flinch of pain. Florence Makororo drew her chair near to mine and bent her head slowly to meet my gaze. Her troubled eyes searched my face for comfort and I felt, all too sharply, her mother's pain.

'I don't know what to do, Amai Zenzele. Somewhere, we did something wrong. When I was growing up, we often ate nothing but mealie porridge and peanuts before bed. We walked four miles to school, only to learn our lessons outside, seated on the red earth in the shade of a mango tree. As soon as I got home, I had to remove my uniform so it could be washed and pressed for the next day; we could not afford to have two. I changed into a faded, three-time hand-me-down dress and walked to the fields to join my mother in planting and sowing. Late in the evening, we returned, only to wash the red dust off our sweaty bodies before we set about gathering wood, collecting pots, preparing *sadza*, frying vegetables and what little meat we were lucky to have for the evening meal. When visitors came, we greeted them properly, we gladly offered and shared what modest refreshments we had in the true communal and Christian spirit that was the very foundation of our lives in the village. It was only late, late after the dishes were cleared, washed and put away, the kitchen was swept and scrubbed, and the water drums had been filled for the next day's baths and cooking – that I found time to sit still with my schoolbooks, using candlelight, mind you, as the only light, for we had none of this electricity, and tried to concentrate and prepare my lessons for the next day. My dear, I had no time for the sort of mischief that our children seek out these days. Ah, no, no. At Christmas, and only Christmas, we received one new dress (which would be our Sunday dress, our party dress and our going-to-town dress) and we had cake after dinner. Those days!' She chuckled softly, shaking her head as if her memories were deceiving her. I laughed too. We had come a long way.

Her eyes grew sad again. As the maid set down a full tray of tea and little puffy scones, Florence got up from her chair and stood by the french windows looking out on to her perfect garden.

'When Independence came, we celebrated with tears in our eyes! The country was ours! We would continue the struggle to ensure that our children received every opportunity of Western privilege. The whites had hoarded the pleasures and advantages of our nation for too long. My God, there were horse-riding and French lessons, video games and trips to London and New York. There was nothing our children asked for that we denied them. We who had grown up knowing only deprivation, austerity and hard labour. We wanted only the best for them. We even sent them to the best private schools with plenty of whites.' The last phrase was uttered with particular disappointment, as if some guarantee had been recanted or some promise broken.

She waved her arms about the sitting room, helplessly. The room was like a museum of African assimilation. On the far wall were shelves of video games, movies and a computer. Above them hung a shiny calendar from B & B Hardware. On the top shelf were scattered trophies and prizes awarded to each of her children for ballet, rugby and tennis, from their prestigious private schools: St George's for the boys and the Dominican convent for the girls. The piano at the rear of the room stood majestic beneath a shiny but dark painting of the wild zebra of the highlands. The nearby coffee tables were cluttered with gaudy souvenirs of every description including a row of gigantic beer mugs from 'Merry England'. The room, with its rich golden carpeting and matching velvet sofas, was the Zimbabwean's version of Western sophistication. The better suburbs of Harare housed no end of replicas of this model.

She resumed speaking. 'But it was all in vain. They have neither respect nor gratitude. When Baba va Stephen's father lived here in the days before he died, you remember how he was in and out of the hospital; it was terrible. Petranella refused to attend to him. Her own grandfather! Her own father's father! She complained that he was decrepit; she lifted not a finger at his funeral in Chakowa. It was a struggle to get her even to go! My mother scolded me for hours about her. She says we have spoiled her. She tells me that these modern children are culturally bleached! That we have not taught them respect or dignity. What can I say to this? How do you teach children integrity, I ask you? I virtually have to beg Petranella to get her to help with little things around the house; she is out with friends all weekend long – we do not see her until the early morning. Even her older bróther, Stephen, a grown man, is in his bed long before her! It is a disgrace! Her father has threatened and punished to no avail. She is smoking and drinking without shame, right here beneath this roof! I would not be surprised if there are even drugs involved. When she is at home she has her radio on full and emerges only for meals and to greet people. These are not the customs that we were taught.' And now her voice began to crack, and I dreaded her next words. It was the nightmare of all African mothers.

'And now she has told me that she is pregnant! How am I to tell her father? Worse still, how do I find the words to tell my own mother my shame? Who will share this heavy burden with me? Ah, me! What heinous evils did I unwittingly commit in my life that God should choose to heap such scorn upon my head? Was I so proud that I need to be the laughing stock of Harare to gain humility? Must I now bear the curse of hearing our good name dragged through the mud, to hear our name in every gossip's mouth? Ah, Amai Zenzele, it is too much for me. As if things were not bad enough, she says that she is not even sure who the father of her child is. Is this our reward for providing the best for her? Is that what she has been up to while we slave day and night to pay for her private-school fees? It is shameful!' Amai Stephen took a tissue from her bag and wiped her eyes. I touched her arm gently. She was my age but I had always perceived her as older, perhaps because her husband was fifteen years our senior. The ancient deference to age dictated by our culture prohibited me from acting on my feelings and embracing her. I had little to say and so I lied with some soothing words. I could not condemn her.

'You cannot blame yourself, Amai Stephen. You have given her so much. One can never be sure what bad influences there are at school. And the television blares all day, glorifying every vice. Our children sit transfixed before the screen soaking in every detail, ready to imitate what they see at the next opportunity. They have no idea of the responsibilities and consequences of their actions – which the telly and the movies happily omit from their scripts. How can you fight these powerful forces? The important thing now is to talk to her about it and decide what is best. Whatever happens, you are her mother and she is your child.'

She shook her head. 'She wants none of my advice. It is as if she is furious with me, when it should be the other way around. He-he, my dear. She is telling me that she can "handle it". Can you imagine! She does not even have a secondary-school education. Now she speaks like a grown woman – as if we were equals!' She shot a sharp glare at the empty hallway. 'Did you see the way she defied me about the tea? Shameless girl! She is spoilt, that is her problem. She is too used to drivers, maids and cooks. I should ship her off to the bush. Maybe then she would understand just how lucky she is. She does not know what it is to work. Children these days think that money grows on trees!' She sank back into her enveloping velvet sofa, drinking the last of her tea. I let her be for several minutes. She suddenly turned to me once again, this time with a spark of hope in her eyes.

'Hey! I have an idea!' she exclaimed, excited now, sitting straight up and placing her hand on my knee. 'Couldn't you persuade Zenzele to spend part of her coming holidays with us in Victoria Falls? It would be so good for Petranella. Zenzele seems so level-headed, I am sure she would listen to her.'

I was startled by this request. But my maternal protective forces surged to my rescue. Why should you do her mother's dirty work? I had no intention of leasing my own daughter out to correct the errant ways of others' children, like a paediatric cultural counsellor. I would not have you discussing abortion, adoption and childbirth for them. Those are issues that they will have to face all by themselves. After all, they had wanted children who were just like those in the West. Well, now they had them, let *them* deal with them! Frankly, the less time you spent with Petranella Makororo, in my opinion, the better. I informed Florence that it was the anniversary of Babamukuru's death, a special occasion for our family. I declined on your behalf.

When I left, it was late. I was burdened by a tremendous sadness. I understood Florence's predicament well. All the peri-Independent generation shared a common vision of a better life. Unfortunately, too many of us had translated this into a material definition of success. We developed all the symptoms of the Post-Colonial Syndrome, endemic to Africa: acquisition, imitation and a paucity of imagination. We simply rushed to secure what the colonialists had. We bought their homes, attended their schools, leased their offices, spoke their language, played their sports, and courted their company. We denied our own culture, relieved to leave our primitive origins far away, in some forgotten village. And so we believed ourselves sophisticated at last, integrated into the mainstream of cosmopolitan culture. We created an invisible white line of ultimate aspiration: to achieve what the Europeans had. This was the epitome of civilization, the very definition of evolutionary advancement. We ceased to dream, to have our own vision of happiness and success. We were able to carry off this farce with aplomb but our children were getting caught in some grey zone that was neither black culture nor truly white either. We had to acknowledge our dual citizenship. We are urban and rural, old and new. We exist in contradictory timeframes; in one we are creating computer programs for artificial intelligence and in another we are carrying a bucket to the river to fetch drinking water. It is our reality; we cannot run away from it. If we cannot fully resolve our dual citizenship as Africans, we must at least be honest with ourselves for the children's sake. It is a commitment that your father and I made when you were born. I could not forsake our determination to expose you to our culture. If in the end you rejected it, that was fine, but we had fulfilled our responsibility as African parents; the rest was up to you.

By now you had finished packing Joy's things. You closed the bag and set it down next to the others. I wanted in some way to share this vision that we had.

'Zenzele, sit down before you go. I know it is late and you are disappointed. But the village is a special place for us. It is full of childhood memories, old friends and familiar haunts. Do you know Auntie Linda and I used to sneak away after our chores on hot December afternoons to bathe in the Umvumvumvu River? We would splash around, playing and screaming. Then we would lie on the rocks at the bank, hidden from view by the thick shrubs, covered by our *jiras*, and make up great stories about the wild animals of the bush. Invariably we fell asleep, then awoke to hear one of the boys calling us. They used to yell at us, "You're going to get it this time.

Mama is furious!" I can never drive over that bridge without a mischievous smile stealing across my face. In the city, sometimes life is a mad rush: it is dashing from home to drop Joy and Tendai at school, fuming in traffic on the way, running from one appointment to the next, making sure the driver picks the children up on time after school, then rushing home to change quickly for some important function in town. It is easy to lose one's priorities in the frantic urban rhythm. Values are misplaced and time is stringently apportioned.' I looked up to see if I was having any impact so far on my audience. Your long fingers were leafing absently through one of Joy's baby picture books. Your lips were pursed in a quivering pout. I continued.

'We do not want our children to grow up thinking that the city is all there is, as if we sprang up from cement pavements and towering high-rises. The city is such a small part of African life; it leaves out so much. Chakowa may look like a dry, dull village to you now but in our day it was magical. Linda and I – well actually it was more Linda's idea than mine – created an underground kingdom beneath the far pillar of the arch of the concrete bridge over the Umvumvumvu River. There was a nook formed by the walls of the thick cement columns, the brambles of the thicket that shaded the river and the rocky ledge that rose sharply above the water's edge. The floor was formed of fat roots of the baobab trees whose sparse branches loomed high above. The roots were plump and fleshy like an old woman's thighs as they dived over the ledge and disappeared into the swirling foam of the river below. I remember the day that Linda discovered the place. She whispered to me late one evening after she was sure Farai was asleep.

'"Sisi Shiri."

'"What is it, Linda? Why aren't you asleep yet?" I whispered, turning my back and sliding down in the bed, away from Farai's elbow.

'"I am too excited, Sisi. I have found a secret place, and if you promise never to take anyone there, I shall show it to you in the morning."

'Indeed, the next morning she performed her chores with such speed and cheerfulness that I was curious to see what geological find could possibly have produced this metamorphosis and account for my sister's unusual behaviour. To get to the spot we had to scurry under the edge of the bridge, crouch down and crawl on all fours for what seemed to be ages and then climb over several precarious-looking rocks to inch along a thorny branch before we finally reached what initially appeared to be a little cave. You must remember that in those days we often romped about without shoes, so it was a most painful journey, although Linda's calloused heels seemed not to feel a thing. It smelled of red clay and rotting leaves. I was not impressed. But Linda soon set to work and coopted me into helping her furnish her little den. Like two little birds building their nest, we foraged about in the thick woodlands that enclosed the river. We collected all sorts of things – like old tins, in which we placed the variegated plants that grew along the river bank. We weaved together a mat from bamboo sticks and even made a few "sofas" from an old mattress that we gouged the fluff out of and covered with a few discarded sheets. After eating the dry powder of the *mauyu* fruit, we would clean the inside and fashion the dry, fuzzy shells into cups and bowls. Linda was brave enough to roll a few rocks in to serve as little tables. I was too terrified – not of the long climb over the sharp ledge but, rather, because I feared the slimy, wiggling green things that squirmed under each rock and crunched as they rolled. Linda only laughed at me – she was absolutely fearless. We made two unsteady shelves from a pile of uneven wood planks and several bricks that we lugged from an abandoned house behind the old mission cemetery. As it grew more habitable, I became en-thusiastic and collected brightly coloured soft-drink bottles and shiny biscuit and tea tins of all shapes and sizes to decorate the shelves. At noon, the sun streamed in through several cracks in the bush. It lit up the room in a rainbow of colours and sparkling shadows as it bounced off the glass and tin. After an intense week, we celebrated by having a private tea party.

'"It is perfect, our own private place. This is our special kingdom. We make the rules. Nobody can come and tell us what to do or make us run away." She beamed.

'And so we had a little refuge beneath the bridge. In the afternoon, it was cool and you could hear the murmurs of the Umvumvumvu River as it flowed past. In the distance, we could hear the splashes and high-pitched laughter of the young women who came to bathe at the river to relieve the heat of the December afternoons. Every time a large lorry or car sped by on the road above us, everything shook like an earthquake. Luckily, in those days there were precious few vehicles. For almost a year, it served as a meeting place for Linda and me, far from the chores of our home and the confines of the village. I read my tattered schoolbooks while Linda played make-believe. She was always pretending to be an emperor or soldier. I think I was closest to my little sister during that year. Of course as I grew older and my responsibilities mounted, my interest waned. I had to concern myself with the concrete and the real. Linda continued to use that hidden spot for years. Soon it became the secret place for her and our cousin Tinawo to meet. In fact, even during the Revolution they used to stash food for the freedom fighters there and once when the Rhodesian army had actually sent out a search party to arrest Linda, she hid there for a solid month. We brought her food, and many comrades over the years learned the secret path to Linda's place. It is a pity it's gone now, for even after I escaped the village and lived in Harare there were times when I longed for the cool solitude it offered. It was burned down many summers ago when a car swerved off the bridge, caught flame and plunged into the river, igniting every branch on its path.

'I used to love to go to town. Baba bought a second-hand car from a fleeing missionary in 1938. We were the first and only family in Chakowa to possess such a contraption. Consequently, it served as an ambulance, taxi, cattle- and horse-trailer, fruit and vegetable delivery truck, school bus and police van. That poor vehicle. It is a wonder it lasted for twenty years. By then, of course, the paint, once a magnificent green, was chipped and flaked. What remained of the front seats was only a spring, the rest having been replaced by home-made cushions crafted from abandoned mattresses and traditional fabric. The back window was smashed and the whole car leaned precariously to the right at all times and most alarmingly at sharp turns. It died exactly one hour after my father did. I remember because we had just loaded it up with blankets and supplies for the funeral, and when my uncle stepped in to start it, it gave an enormous metallic sigh, then grew deathly quiet and never made another sound. While it lived, however, whenever anyone in the village was taken ill, the sister from the clinic would come running down the hill to our house to beg Baba to take them to Mutare General Hospital. In fact, the Manese twins were born on the back seat of that old car. At harvest time the neighbours brought gourds filled with fire-red tomatoes, baskets of sunny mangoes, sacks and sacks of beans and potatoes for Baba to take into the market square. The car itself was a constant source of wonder to the villagers. Whenever they saw us coming, in a dusty red haze, they would leap out of its path, only to jostle each other to file along the sideline and wave frantically at us, as if we were in some kind of parade. Farai, my youngest sister, was the first to call it a "grasshopper", but before long the entire village referred to the car as "the grasshopper".

'My father often allowed us to accompany him on his various errands. I would sit crouched on the front seat, with my head high and my knees tightly buckled below me, so as not to touch the gearbox as we bumped along the pothole-ridden road from Chakowa to Mutare. When Linda came too and there was no other baggage, we would sit in the back and play games. Our favourite was to count the number of baboons in the bush as we sped by. The one with the least sightings had to give the other all of her sweets, which Baba invariably bought us at Mr Malawi's Bazaar at the end of the day. Naturally, if you spotted a zebra or elephant, then you automatically won. As you can imagine, this was not a very objective game and we often fought bitterly about the sightings.

'I loved to see the shops full of pretty things. I was always happy to mind the car which meant that I could nestle on the back seat and watch the whites in their spotless starched clothes clip-clop past. Early on I noticed the difference between us and them. Their clothes never had a stain or a hole in them, and their hemlines were sharp and straight. As a child, I was particularly fascinated by their shoes. For one thing, they

23

matched perfectly and the strings of their shoelaces stayed put neatly in their holes instead of cutting through them and becoming all shredded and unravelled, so that in order to tie one's shoes one had to crisscross the laces unevenly in the remaining holes. Secondly, their shoes were shiny, not dusty and worn. More wondrous still, they actually seemed to fit their feet instead of pinching or flopping about like the Africans' shoes did. At that time I thought they must have better cobblers, tailors and shinier irons and that if we went to the European shops we would all have such a smart look. But we were forbidden to enter those stores by large signs that hung crookedly from the doorknobs. Even those of us who could not yet read knew what the signs meant. Years later, long after I learned to read the "Whites Only" signs, I understood that the differences were deep and that poverty and imperialism were what put the holes and stains on our clothing and kept them off theirs.

'Mr Bright Malawi was one of my father's closest friends. He owned a general store across from the bus terminal. No matter the errand or the hour, we always stopped at his lively bazaar before returning home. Outside, its stucco walls were animated by the brightly coloured smiles of a young African couple sharing a bubbly soft drink and rugged American cowboys smoking cigarettes. Inside, it was dim and smelled of a mixture of the dried goat meat that hung in strips from the rafters and the many spices that were arranged row upon row behind the counter. The shop was cluttered with every item imaginable. He stocked soap, batteries, blankets, flour, school uniforms, underwear, pens, live chickens and cooking pots. For our purposes, however, his most noteworthy merchandise was the outstanding selection of lollipops and chewing gum. We would raid the jars of sweets that filled the glass counter beneath the bright-red cash register while the two old men sat at the back table sharing a cool beer and discussing business and church matters. Often I went alone with my father for the boys were still young and Linda more often than not detested going to town. First and foremost, she objected to getting all dressed up for the occasion. Linda was worse than an enraged cat, clawing and screeching when I tried to brush her dense curls into a neat bun to render her presentable.

"'Leave me alone! I don't want to go!" she would sob.

'I only managed to talk her into it, from time to time, by inventing all sorts of games for the journey. I once asked her why she did not enjoy going. Naturally, I suspected that she was just being lazy. Baba always needed our help to carry the market goods, assist the sick into the hospital wards or run into the shops to buy something. Sometimes he just asked us to sit and mind the car. She claimed, however, that town was "stuffy".

"'It's horrible. Baba is always telling us that we cannot go in there, that we cannot walk here, that we are not allowed to buy this or that. I would rather play alone by the river. There I can shout or sing or laugh or run, and I can take anything I want from the woods to play and do anything I want in my secret place," she said, pouting. Of course, then she had been too young to understand that our father was simply doing as the signs said. But she was a child of the open fields and she felt suffocated by the strict racial confinement of the city. It is funny how little children can intuitively understand so much. As usual we reacted antithetically. I was delighted to watch and follow, feeling detached. My sister, however, felt actively restrained, as if *her* personal freedoms, rather than those of the nation as a whole, were being infringed upon. Once the war started, we were no longer allowed to ride along. The boys who worked for us were the only ones permitted to go with Baba. It was no longer fun, anyway. Everyone was sombre and scuttled in and out of shops in a nervous, directed fashion. At every turn we were frisked and searched. You couldn't even buy sweets without having the whole bag turned inside out by the unsmiling security officer at the door and each sweet inspected as if it had a miniature bomb in it. And the curfew made it dangerous to drive in the evenings. We were banished from playing our little game because as the animals became scarce and the soldiers more numerous, we adapted our game to see how many soldiers and how many freedom fighters we could spot. Needless to say, our pointing and crying out was not welcomed by either group and once got us fired at. It was after that trip that we lost all interest (and Baba sternly forbade us from going into town).

'But the point is that you will never know the gay abandon of jumping into the Umvumvumvu River to bathe or come face to face with a baby hare or a wide-eyed baboon while playing in the bush. And, thank God, you will never know the pains that come from walking in the wild without shoes or the aches of working all day in the fields. Nevertheless, at least you can somehow be a part of my past – of our past, which lives on in Chakowa. Things are still as they were there, and they are so different from this. The air, the way of treating one another, and even the food are different here.'

By now, you were turned towards me, looking in-tently into my face. Finally, I was getting somewhere! I continued, observing you from a more discreet angle as I put the last few things in the bag.

'In the rural areas the mangoes are bigger [a smile], the *sadza* is better [a rolling of the eyes], the tea has more flavour [a nod] and *matumbu* tastes real [a grimace].'

You crossed your feet and looked up at me. The lips were struggling to contain some witty remark, not wanting to give in too readily.

'That is why everyone there is so fat!' Your lips exploded now, wide open, and your body was shaking with laughter. I laughed, too. The storm was over.

'It is also important for us to take care of Mbuya,' I added.

'Mama, why doesn't she just come and live here with us? Her life would be so much easier.'

'Heh. That would be the day! She has sworn on the grave of her departed parents that she will never leave Chakowa. She and Babamukuru James built that home from nothing. She will tell you how she chased away baboons, killed snakes, and ploughed that land to make it home. She is too proud to leave Chakowa. Besides, she goes to Babamukuru's grave every morning to sweep away the fallen leaves and bird droppings, to clear old flowers, lay a fresh bouquet of wild flowers and chase away stray animals that shelter there. She would never leave him. And you know how she is. She cares deeply for your father, who is her favourite son, and all of us, but she treasures her independence. She detests idleness. After one day sitting around our house, she is like a caged bird.'

'Do you remember the last time she came in to see the orthopaedist about her knees and Baba insisted she stay the weekend? By the time we came back from town, just a few hours after her appointment, she was long gone on a bus back east so she could water her beans and maize in time.' You were shaking your head as you said this, laughing still.

'And nothing pleases her more than having that house chock-full of her brood,' I continued. 'She bustles about and boasts to her neighbours. She will call out on every side as she leads a gaggle of grandchildren to the shops, "Oh, Amai Chiwere, I will not be by for tea today. The house is full of little ones – just look at them. The family is here, grandchildren and all. I am exhausted! Come along, children." Then on Sundays, to make Amai Tawona green with jealousy, "Oh! Good afternoon, Patience, my friend. Do you mind if we take this shortcut through your path? I am taking them to the Easter play at the church. Just look at this pretty dress they bought me. The entire clan has descended upon me once again. I had nothing to feed them – you know how times are hard these days, especially after last season's drought. He-he, but no matter! They came with that big, fancy car loaded down with meat, wine, cakes and biscuits and other things that I cannot even pronounce, he-he. Yowe! *Here hamuna we.* Others would stay in the city, feeling important, but not this lot! They never fail to come home. Never a holiday in peace for an old woman! He-he. Say *morowe* to Granny Patience, children." Then with a smug smile and a hearty wave she would shout her parting shot: "Come by later for tea: we could never finish all of that food alone!"

'Granny Patience is a sad, lonely old woman. Her children send for her once a year to come to Harare, only to sit in an overstuffed chair and watch television. I know that she detests the indignity of it, but her pride would not allow her to stay in the country all year round. Tongues would grow loose to see a proud old woman with so many educated children living in the capital city, their houses sprawling with empty, airy rooms, living in her thatched hut and never visiting. It was important for Granny Patience to show that she had relations who were "high up". So once a year she would sigh, tie together her few, faded possessions, and endure the three-hour bus ride to Harare and return one week later, looking paler, thinner and even more cheerless than when she had left. She always loudly claimed, for all to hear, that her children spoiled her terribly, but her appearance belied the truth. The children who perfunctorily sent for her had little time in their fast-paced city lives for the sluggish and obsolete. Her peasant superstitions and labourer's odours evoked unpleasant memories best forgotten. They have set foot back in the village only twice since they left as children – once for their father's funeral and once when Amai Tawona (as we call Granny Patience) was ill. When Mbuya was a young mother, Amai Tawona used to laugh at her for educating her children, especially the girls. Amai Tawona used to wear new dresses each Sunday. With virtually all her seven children working in the fields all day, she was able to plant and reap one of the largest harvests in the village. But she did not know that she had simultaneously also sowed the seeds of discontent and resentment from her children, which she reaps today. She had lived for the present, for a new hat, a more elegant pair of gloves, for those pretty new curtains. Mbuya and Babamukuru, meanwhile, ploughed their investments in the hearts and minds of their children. And today they are yielding large returns. Today your Tete Murielle is a doctor, your father is a lawyer and your uncle, Babamunini Arthur, is a professor at the university. Had it not been for Mbuya's foresight, Tete Murielle would probably be changing the nappies of some European baby in the suburbs, as is the fate of most of our uneducated rural girls, and your father and uncle would be garden boys and cook boys. According to our custom, one generation takes care of the other. If we followed Amai Tawona's example, we would soon be putting away our old, with all their wisdom and love, in those dreadful nursing homes of the so–called civilized world. Some countries create whole villages of the senile and lame so that they do not interfere with the hustle and bustle of daily commerce. I suspect, even more importantly, the aged are hidden away so that we do not remember that one day we shall all walk that path, that we shall one day grow slow and stooped.'

The long fingers covered your floppy mouth as it stretched into a yawn. I felt relieved when we said goodnight. If my memory is true, I think you will agree that it was one of our best holidays in Chakowa.

III

There are many aspects of our culture that you find difficult to accept. I know that you have often bewailed the nefarious links of our clan. Even after years of great mental effort, I myself often fail to make the correct connections. Do you remember how disappointed you were two years ago to discover that a new acquaintance, on whom you had a 'serious crush', was your close cousin? You hissed in exasperation, 'But, Mama, is there anyone in this city that I am not related to? Each time I meet someone they turn out to be Grandfather's uncle's niece's cousin or something! It is impossible!' We laughed so, because it was true. More perplexing still are the hierarchy and customs attached to each specific relationship in our ubiquitous family tree. It will take time but you will learn. As my daughter it will be your responsibility to maintain those links for all of us. Do not be discouraged by its breadth. Therein lies its beauty; there is always someone new to meet, a new friend, a business acquaintance, a confidante, an infinite source of advice and support. The extended family is your community, your own emotional, financial and cultural safety net. It is Africa's most powerful resource.

I shall never forget how militant you were when the issue of *lobola* came up.

'I will never be bought! Mama, how could you possibly accept some cattle and cash in exchange for my freedom?' You gave me a look of such reproof one would have thought that I had just put in a bid to sell you into slavery.

'It is not a purchase, Zenzele. It is an expression of appreciation of how well we have brought you up.'

'In that case you won't get much,' you interjected, bursting into laughter.

'I am being serious, Zenzele. You must not take the Western anthropologists' view of our culture. They perceive our customs through their lens. There are terms and customs that cannot be translated adequately into their language and so become distorted. *Lobola* is called a "bride price", kings are "chiefs", our medicine is called "witchcraft", and our religion is labelled "animist". They do not capture the spirit of our culture. We are at fault also. Even our own people have sullied the beauty of our customs. For example, Amai Patience accepted a money order of five thousand pounds wired in from London by her Nigerian fiancé! She never even saw the fellow! That is appalling and transgresses a girl's dignity completely. To him no doubt, he has simply paid for her. But according to tradition, there is an elaborate ceremony that brings the two families together and the future groom pays tribute to his fiancée and her parents.'

'Mama, you are defending a custom that identifies women as property, transferred from father to husband. It is dreadful. I shall have none of it.'

'You cannot reject a custom simply because it is vulnerable to abuse. That is like not going to church because there are so many hypocrites there. The important thing is that you understand the meaning of it and abide by it.'

You were not swayed. 'Never, Mama.' I was running out of energy and arguments.

'It is our custom, Zenzele. Westerners give rings, we have *lobola*.'

'Well then, I am not going to marry an African. I shall marry in America – some dreadfully clever blond-haired creature who has never even heard of Africa. We shall be married on a boat and sail around the world for a honeymoon! Afterwards we shall settle on his huge ranch and I shall drive one of those enormous American cars!'

I looked up in alarm. Your lips were quivering with audacity, then tensed in a vain attempt to suppress your laughter.

'Honestly, Zenzele, you watch too much television. You do not know what you are saying. An intercultural marriage is difficult and fraught with compromise.'

'But free of *lobola*.'

My exasperation must have been evident, for you sat still for several minutes settling your mirth, rallying your intelligence. That is how I often saw you: multiple personalities at your disposal. In any situation, you would select the most fitting one and metamorphose before our eyes.

'I hear your point, Mama. You have often explained that *lobola* is the appreciation of the gifts that a woman brings to her marriage. I find it encouraging that our culture actually places great value on an educated, smart woman who has a career. I heard that Thandi's *lobola* was tripled after she became a lawyer. I have also heard the argument that it is to thank the parents for all that they have done for their daughter. I suppose if submission was

33

the goal, then they would certainly go for the rural, illiterate girls. But it is just difficult for me to appreciate sometimes. I suppose in the old days when everyone understood it all, it worked. But nowadays, when people start sending cheques in the mail or using credit cards for *lobola*, as if they are paying for a pack of beer or a phone bill, then I find it indecent. It is also horrid for men to beat their wives, abuse them or make demands because they feel they bought them. It's in the papers every day. A man and his wife have a quarrel and he beats her senseless. When those so-called traditional courts ask him what gives him the right, his self-righteous excuse is, "I bought her." Why, he can even quote the amount! That's just too much. What is a woman worth, after all? And who has the right to make such an audacious calculation?'

You stood up, shaking your head sorrowfully.

'And do you know what else truly bothers me about our culture?'

I braced myself for another round.

'One minute, Zenzele. How about another cup of tea?' I was stalling for time. So many questions. No answers. Unfortunately for me you missed not a syllable as you prepared the tea.

'Why are women known by their children? Why is Professor Marimba known as Amai Farai? As if no matter what she does she is a housewife first and foremost. As if her only identifiable contribution to mankind was the act of childbirth.'

'But men are also known as such. Mr Marimba is called Baba Farai and Professor Makororo is known as Baba va Stephen. Why, even your own father is called Baba va Zenzele, after his illustrious firstborn.'

'Mama, seriously. That's true, but not as much. It is

just that there are so many things that I do not under-stand. Why do women change their names when they get married, Mama? Professor Marimba, for example. It was the Marodzi family that raised her, sent her to school and put her through university. But she sud-denly becomes not Professor Marodzi but Marimba. I don't get it, Mama. She was born a Marodzi, wasn't she? Why should she or I give up the name we have had all our lives when our husbands do not? *Who* made us the accommodating gender? Men have stability and constancy in their identity. If you are born Mazvita Allen Maseko you remain Mazvita Allen Maseko until you die. Not so for a woman. No indeed. Our names must be a reflection of our relationship to this constant other, as if our own identity were not enough. It must be supplemented by husband, child and family, first Mrs So-and-So, then Amai So-and-So.'

Happily for me, you were no longer expecting a reply. Your face was aglow and you were passionately stirring the sugar into your tea. I sipped the cup you handed me, sitting back comfortably now, happy to relinquish the role of mother and assume my favourite role as audience.

'And have you ever wondered why cat-calling and other public nuisances are not against the law? Sure, call the police when a neighbour's party is disturbing your sleep. They rush over to close down the merrymakers. But if some greasy, dishevelled man is disturbing your peace of mind, cat-calling – "Hey, shooga, wanna ride?" – or even if they whisper obscene insults or follow you for a spell, well it is just a joke! A compli-ment, even! Not a single policeman would take you seriously. Can you imagine going up to one of those patrol cars and complaining that some man was making indecent remarks? We cannot allow such blatant injustice to go on, Mama!'

I sighed, feeling outdated as you continued your feminist litany. My tea was cold now. The sun was shining into the kitchen as it so often does on summer mornings. It was the call of a new day. As a young mother, I had treasured those moments before anyone else awoke. The kitchen was my world. I could make sense of things there. The pretty blue antique china, my neat set of spotless appliances, the coffee, the crockery and fruit arranged just so in the fruit bowl – all had their precise places according to my own system. I had no answers to your questions, which dropped like little bombs to disturb my orderly, swept, waxed and shiny world. Ever since you had burst into womanhood with your fervent egalitarianism and sweet idealism, the complacent foundation of my morning reveries had been shattered. Now I descended every morning to an apparently unending quest to uncover every inconsistency of modern society. I started my day faced with 'Mama, why is it that?', 'Mama, whoever said that things have to be this way?' And that final exasperated, 'Why, Mama, why?' It was no use patiently to explain in that high, adult tone that this was simply the way that the world is and, furthermore, is likely to remain. I had learned that lesson quite early on, when you were about eleven years old. I made such a response then, throwing in a few big words to emphasize my grown-upness and subsequent greater experience and knowledge. But this did not squash your earnestness in the least: you persisted with your questions, undaunted by my rebuff. I did, however, earn a withering stare, with scorn welling up like tears from the deep brown depths of those penetrating eyes of yours, and, worse, that restless mouth furrowed and rolled into a disdainful curl, set off by two defiant dimples on each cheek. After that I did my best to counter your precocious Utopian curiosity. As I sat musing, staring into my cup, part of me snapped. What's in a name, what difference does it make if Katie is called Mai Farai, Professor Marodzi or Professor Marimba? She is the same person. But deep down I knew it did.

I had accepted without question to be Mrs Shungu, to leave my home and family and be a wife. Indeed, it had seemed an honour, a dream come true. How envious all my friends had been at my hen party! I had understood that I was to furnish the home, prepare the meals, ensure that the children were fed, clothed, educated and well kept. It was a challenge that I took on with alacrity. I never asked anyone why I had to be the one to fetch you from the school play, to call your teacher if there was a problem, or to fix your lunches. And now with my tight Afro sprinkled with grey, I finally believed, seeing you grow, that I had achieved something. Surely I had earned the right to sit comfortably in my soft chair and fold my arms with satisfaction, knowing that I had played out my role with grace. I had fulfilled society's expectations and my duties as a woman. And there you were – clever and talented – the very fruit of my labours, challenging my assumptions, making me feel inadequate and obsolete.

What can I say to you? Mine is to make clean, to smooth and comfort. I have done this. I have put my whole life into it. But those Mother Earth eyes of fossil depth tell me it is not enough. The answers you seek are yours to find. I have made my contribution. I have nothing more to add. It is up to your generation to carry us the rest of the way. That was all I could think then. It was a difficult day for me. I spent the entire afternoon ironing, in a vain attempt to smooth out the terrible inconsistencies of our lives.

Two weeks later, on a cool Sunday afternoon, sitting on the back veranda, sipping tall Malawi shandies after a game of tennis, you resumed your musings as if the conversation had never been interrupted. It was one of those perfect days in Harare, bright sunshine, a gentle breeze, not too hot, with clear blue sky above. The garden was alive with the rainbow of pinks, reds and yellows of the rose bushes, the green of Samuel's well-trimmed garden, the lavender of the jacaranda trees whose fragrance wafted through the patio and into the sitting room where your father had fallen asleep with the *Herald* perched atop his newly protuberant belly. The boys were out playing rugby and Joy was at Tete Murielle's for the day. Poor woman – being a doctor was one thing, but spending a day babysitting my manic five-year-old was quite another, as she was fast discovering. Nevertheless, God bless her, she continued to volunteer to take Joy out every other weekend. Tete Murielle always returned those evenings with her clinical cool slightly frazzled. Joy, of course, was still skipping, singing and hopping along, full of energy. I closed my eyes to appreciate fully the blissful quiet of the empty house and the indistinguishable murmurs of the trees as the wind sent their bushy arms waving to and fro.

'Good game, Mama. But it was a bit unfair. You were practising while I was away at school.' The clinking of the ice cubes as you shook your empty glass suddenly stopped. I cautiously opened my eyes. You projected such a penetrating and quizzical look that I

38

knew another little bomb was about to explode. I quickly shut them again, opting to remain in my tranquil darkness.

'Mama, what do you think it means to be an African woman?' I kept my eyes closed for several seconds. I saw my mother now, skin burnt to a charcoal black so that even the few wrinkles didn't show. She had beautiful smooth skin. I found it odd that no matter where or how often she was bruised by a fall, or burned while cooking at the fire, or cut by the barbed-wire pen as she fed the chickens, no matter what the injury, my mother's skin retained no blemishes. In a few days, all was miraculously healed. I sincerely believed that she had some way of regenerating herself. Her spirit was the same way. No matter what the insult to her pride and integrity, her spirit remained as generous and impenetrably pragmatic as ever.

I think of what would have been her answer. But I know. Even though as a girl I never questioned such things, I am as certain of her opinion as if she had written a treatise on the matter. There was no time then for such abstract musings. She would have raised up her thick muscular arms as she often did and replied: 'Do you see these hands? These are my words and their work is my testimony. Your words are your deeds.' She had once told me, 'There is no place in a woman's world for your foolish fancies.' (I had told her that I wanted to take her on a long journey somewhere far away to see other lands.) 'To be an African woman means to work hard,' she said. The rest was spoken most eloquently by those hands. She stood as a formidable testimony to her own truth. At dawn she arose, said her prayers, and began her day before the sun could signal it so. She fed the goats and chickens; she fetched water; she prepared breakfast; she collected wood. All day she washed, scrubbed and ironed. Late in the afternoon, I would meet her coming from the family farm plot on my way home from school. In the evening, before bed, when all was put away, she would kneel down and thank God for another day done. She seemed so complete then. Yet the next day the entire cycle started afresh. There was a new load of washing to do, another pile of dishes, mouths to be fed, animals to be tended. She approached every day with the same fervour and passion with which you approach your social revolution. Her silent industriousness was so convincing that I came to believe that she was the very epitome of the African woman – until, of course, you came along. Never still, always questioning, moulding the world around you rather than trying to fit into some niche that was predestined according to your race and gender, you shattered my image to pieces. I no longer know what or who is the African woman. Perhaps she is some synthesis of you both. I reluctantly opened my eyes, shielding them from the bright sun with one hand.

'It is to be strong, Zenzele. It is to be at peace within. You must always listen to that inner voice and not permit others to drown it out. It is to measure your words; to balance your works with your gifts carefully; it is in some ways to be selfless, to serve others yet to know and defend your rights to the bitter end. Remember that it was an African woman, Mbuya Nehanda, who launched Zimbabwe's struggle for independence when she waged the war on the British South African Company in the 1890s. Imagine Cleopatra and Nefertiti. Look at our women in southern Africa. The schoolgirls of Soweto, the fighters of Maputo, the *mjibas*, the young freedom fighters in Zimbabwe – strong, heroic women who found the balance between cause, culture and self. Being an African woman is what you will make of it, Zenzele. But never forget that for the majority, it also means to rise out of bed before others, to make the cold kitchen warm, to work the fields in the blazing heat, to walk for miles on dusty paths carrying water on your head, wood under your arms and a baby on your back.'

To my great surprise, your expression glowed approval. It was one of the few times I left you speechless! I knew it could not last long, so I gathered the rackets and headed in to wake your father for lunch.

I remember on the eve of my wedding, as I was nervously trying on my dress for the twentieth time, your father's mother slipped into my bedroom and locked the door. In the olden days, a woman returned to her parents' home, where the wedding took place. And so I had dutifully arrived in Chakowa three days earlier to begin preparations for the feasting and dancing that would precede and follow the traditional ceremonies. I was already uneasy, but the appearance of my mother-in-law-to-be at that hour fixed me in a state of catatonic terror. She stood at the door, stooped over her cane, robed in a bright floral flannel nightgown, her grey hair bundled in a majestic headdress, and simply stared at me. She did not smile or move for a full two minutes. Then she hobbled to my side and, taking my hand, guided me to the bed.

'Come, my child. Sit down. I have something to show you.' My head reeled. I had had so little private contact with her to this point. She was notorious for being a stubborn, cantankerous old woman whose displeasure could be amply displayed but not readily allayed. On that night especially, I wanted nothing to go amiss. I was petrified that, like so many mothers-in-law, she was

41

going to offer me herbs or charms for fidelity, desire or fertility. What would I do? How could I gently but firmly decline the offer without appearing like an uppity city girl? I looked about desperately, wondering where Linda was; she was, after all, supposed to be helping fit the dress – but as usual my little sister was nowhere to be found when I needed her. To my horror and surprise the old lady began to unbutton her gown. Slowly and painfully, the gnarled, arthritic hands began to reveal what was better left hidden. Before I looked away in embarrassment, I caught a glimpse of her breasts, pendulous and glistening but shrivelled like giant black prunes, hanging from her bony frame.

'Now, you have the beauty of youth, so you can shudder at my wrinkled breasts,' she said, chuckling to herself. Her grin was accentuated by a few remaining teeth hanging from thick, pink-and-brown-speckled gums. I was now at an utter loss as to how to respond to her. She continued: 'But just you wait and see, as the seasons pass, your waist shall grow thicker, your hips shall be round and full like the moon, and your breasts will hang low like fruit that has passed its ripeness on the tree.' Now her breasts were fully exposed, I was trying to look away yet not offend. She clasped my right hand in hers. Then she laid it on her wrinkled cheeks and made me caress each crevice. I could feel the roughness of her face, the soft bristles of her eyebrows and the undulations of her forehead as she guided my hand gently over her entire profile. As she did so she spoke softly.

'That wrinkle was from the tears I shed at his birth. *Here hamuna we!* It was painful. It hurt like the lightning that splits the trees. It made me want to sing and cry all at the same time. Right there – that line was when he began to talk. Oh, how I laughed and laughed! That furrow

42

there – yes there – feel how deep that is. That was when he left the farm and joined the struggle. Dear God, how I worried. Oh, and that little crease, that is from grinning at the sweet memory of his success. And that one – ooh, it hurts still there; don't press so deep – that was when they threw him into the jail, and they beat him because he tried to defend the boys who were fighting for our freedom.' She sighed so deeply, I thought she was going to cry. But she only shook her head sadly and slipped my hand down her leathery skin to enfold her breast.

'This is where the strength of your man comes from. This is where he would crawl, grabbing at my blouse, howling for milk. I breast-fed six children, my dear! All greedy and strong. He-he.' She rubbed them gently. I was grateful when she let my hands go and began to cover herself.

'You look at us old women, covered from head to toe in our tight headdresses and our long skirts, and you think we are like the nuns, afraid to show their bodies because it is a sin. But that is not so. It is because we understand nature's ways. We have lived long and deep in the bush with her. And she is a woman like us. My beauty is here now,' she said, pointing to her wrinkles and her breasts. 'There are birthmarks and then there are these. He-he. These are the marks of life. My face, just as it is, the map of my toils and joys, is as precious to me as your little waist and your rounded breasts are to you. This is testimony to the love I have given my family. There is not a mark here that is my own. It belongs to Baba va Tapiwa, Chipo, Farai, Tawona and Ziyanai. It is a body of love. You see it as an old, dry, lifeless thing but one day you shall understand that each beauty has its season. The flaky, rough coconut protects the flesh and the sweet juices within. The body of youth knows its day and must live it to its fullest. The body of the harvest, too, has its time. That is mine. It is a body that has reaped and sown and gathered unto itself. Some day, too, will come the body of the earth, the final eternal one, which has no form or end, to which we must all return. I came to see you tonight, daughter, to tell you these words that my mother-in-law told me on my wedding night ages ago, so that the wisdom of our ancestors may swell and ripen with each new bud that flowers. So our roots grow deeper and our words never die.' At the mention of those deceased, she crossed herself and sat silent for a moment. As she began to fasten her clothes, she whispered on in a more cheerful voice.

'She told me as I sat frightened like a mouse, just like you, "A woman's body follows the moon. It is not still and hard like a man's. Her happiness and sadness take many forms; each day the brightness of her light and the mysterious depths of her shadows may change. A woman is close to the earth yet near to the heavens. She grows like the harvest, she becomes ripe like fruit. When, after many children, my son looks at you and asks where is the beauty of your youth, tell him these words. The body of your youth stays with your youth and the body of the harvest, that is the body of your later years. Look at nature, how she dresses herself for every season. In the summer she adorns herself as fields of rose and pink blooms, with fruits of peach, mango and lemon, and as the season cools, she too dresses in darker hues of brown, maroon and gold, and in the rains she is all grey mist and stormy blues. A woman must always be proud and look after herself." Those are principles we follow forever, even us old ones.' At that she began to cackle loudly. She tapped her cane on the floor and rose with a heave.

44

'Goodnight, my dear girl. You will make my son happy, I know, and you will be a daughter we can be proud of.' And with that, she unlocked my door, took my candle, and left me in complete darkness. I was stunned. I was at once charmed by the beauty of her words and frightened by their meaning. There was something of an honour in the intimacy of transcending the barriers erected by pride, decorum and custom. She had shown off her body as a magnificent monument of the human spirit over hardship. How I wished then that my body too, if it had to droop and shrivel, for surely everyone's did, would furl and dessicate with grace to sculpt the victory of my spirit: that I, too, when heavy and bent with age, could caress my wrinkled lids and hold my sagging flesh as a majestic robe of a life well lived.

I slept not a wink. It was the first time that I was happy to be squashed in the crowded bed with Linda on my right and Farai at my left. It felt safe there. It felt natural somehow to return to Chakowa, even though at that point I had been out on my own in Mutare for several years. This new world to come, of marriage and motherhood, was so very, very new. It was too bewildering to contemplate. Everyone, it seemed, from my mother to your father's mother, had their own definition of what it meant to be a woman. And as I lay there feeling Linda's warm breath on my cheek, I knew that somehow we all had to find our own way, our own words, our own season.

IV

You once asked me, 'Mama, didn't you ever want to go to London to study, or live in Paris for a while?' I shook my head and said nothing that day. I did not want to frighten or disillusion you, but now it seems fitting to tell you my reasons. To be sure, the Western world is enchanting. I have been dazzled by the neon blaze of fluorescent city lights that render the moon a pale, primitive bulb. I have stood mouth agape at the architectural splendours of centuries ago that house their grand salons, theatres and operas. And I have abandoned myself in the mazes of shops resplendent with any item that the human mind can imagine and money can buy. It is a satiated world of genius and decadence. It is easy to get lost there. Thousands never return. They are lost to that dreaded black hole, the 'brain drain'. Do you remember Mukoma Byron, my cousin whom I have mentioned from time to time? You were too young when he visited to remember.

Mukoma Byron was one of my favourite childhood playmates; he often came to our compound to help mother and me with our chores. He was exceptionally bright at school. His nickname was 'Watt', because those few who had electricity knew that a lightbulb's power and intensity are measured in watts. He was popular because of his easy wit and charm. When he won the Umtali East Methodist Missionary scholarship to go to Oxford and study medicine, the entire village celebrated. Butcher Madimba killed a cow and two goats for the occasion and Mbuya Chidakwa (I think that was an alias though) brewed twelve pots of her most potent traditional beer. It was as if the circus had come to our village. A reporter came from the *Rhodesian Herald* to take Mukoma Byron's photograph! He was a national celebrity, proclaimed his mother. Mbuya Makoni, or Auntie Mai Byron, as we called her, was so proud of him. We raised the money to buy a suitcase at the primary school where he had been an exemplary pupil. Fortunately, he had very few clothes so we were able to get a small one. Sekuru Isaac donated his wool overcoat, which his employer, Sir Winthrop Barningsmith Woods, had given to him in gratitude for ten years of exceptional service. For the cold English winters, I gave him a scarf that I had been knitting, and the church bought him two brand new pairs of shoes. On the day of his departure I accompanied him to the market square to catch the first bus to Harare, in order to get the early flight to London. No one in our village had ever been on a plane before, and Mukoma Byron now assumed the stature of those 'who rub shoulders with white men'. It was still dark when we arrived at the station, but already the market women were laying out their wares, calling out to each other as they worked. The Harare buses were not yet in so we sat on a ledge, exhausted from our long walk.

'I will write to you, little one,' he said affectionately. Needless to say, we always spoke in Shona. English was awkward for us; when we spoke it, it felt like a fizzy drink had gone down funny and all the bubbles were popping up your nose.

'I am sure you shall be very busy, Mukoma. But if you would find the time it would please me very much.' He looked very sombre and I could feel that his body was tense.

'Are you not excited to be going on a big bird far away from here?' I asked incredulously.

'I am frightened, Shiri. I have never left this village. It is all I know. And how can I leave my poor mother? Who will take care of her? And who will cut the wood for my little sister, Shiri?' I smiled shyly, pleased that he would miss me. He was the only one who called me by my nickname in that soft way, so that it actually sounded like a little sparrow in flight. He had given me that name himself because he teased that I had the appetite of a bird. I leaned a little closer, timidly, to comfort him.

'We will be all right, Mukoma Byron. Do not worry. You shall do your mother so much more good by becoming a famous doctor. When you return, you can buy her a big house with running water and a cooking fire inside! I promise that I shall go and see her every day. I will look after her for you, Mukoma Byron, I promise. Oh! Here is your bus.' I choked on the last few words. My tongue felt thick now and my lips quivered. A rickety blue bus lurched towards us, spewing clouds of black fumes as it passed. It stopped just ahead of us, and as we approached we could discern the bright reds and blues of an advertisement that was painted all over it. He took the little bag that I had been carrying, gave me a warm hug, and boarded. I walked to his window. I was crying now.

'Be a good girl, Shiri. Save your tears for the dead and the ugly! I am neither! Study hard, Shiri, so that you can join me soon.' I could not answer; I only bobbed my head.

'I will write as soon as I arrive and every week!' He was shouting now as the bus revved its engine and drove off to town to pick up the bulk of its passengers. I waved frantically but was obscured by the darkness of the early dawn and the black fumes of the bus's exhaust.

He kept his word for the first few years. He wrote regular, disturbing, troubled letters. I knew he was not happy yet I was too overwhelmed by the strangeness of his letters to be able to be of any use. So, I filled my letters with news of the village and my progress in school. He longed to come home: it was too cold, too fast and too alien. Gradually the pages dwindled from five to three, then to one, and eventually I received the occasional postcard from cities with such impossible names, like Düsseldorf, Glasgow and Aix-en-Provence, which I had to look up in the school atlas. There were no more of the searching questions such as 'Shiri, have you ever wondered what it actually means to be an African?' or, 'What is the true meaning of life, Shiri?' Then came the rumours that he had failed and dropped out of Oxford. A cousin of Sekuru Isaac claimed that he had taken to drinking heavily. One of Tete Murielle's colleagues swore that he had seen him waiting at tables in an East End pub during his last visit. The latest was that he had become a cook for wealthy English nobility and was living with a fellow house servant.

His mother would storm whenever she heard the stories. 'Lies! That is nonsense! Slander! Jealous people are making up stories to pain me. My son is bright and hardworking. He will come one day as a doctor and all these stupid peasants will come here and eat their words! Just you wait and see.' She prayed for God to guide him and give him strength daily. Whenever she received the occasional money order she proclaimed triumphantly to the entire village, 'You see how good and generous my Byron is. Even with his small scholarship he saves in order to send a little gift to his poor old mother.'

The four years stretched to six, then ten. I got married and moved away. Auntie Mai Byron wrote long letters begging him to come home and set up his practice here; she told him that she grew old and longed to see him settled with a family. His responses eventually ceased altogether, but the cheques continued to come more regularly and became larger as the years went by. The poor old woman grew sick and despondent. She would complain bitterly to me whenever I saw her, 'What do I care for money when I can cook my *sadza* and grow my beans? I want my child.'

The rumours continued, but people took pity on the old woman and never said a word to her or any of his family. Until I moved away, I kept my word to Mukoma Byron. I took care of his mother and went to see her every day. Even when we moved, first to Mutare and then Harare, I have made a point to visit once every two weeks and I instructed the boys who worked for my mother to visit her each day.

It was fifteen years before Mukoma Byron finally came home. After a silence of almost ten years I received a brief telegram: 'Arriving Air Rhodesia, Friday 21 November. Please come. Regards. Byron Makon.'

I chuckled over the last name. It was just like the Brits to leave off the 'i'. They had such difficulty with foreign names!

I did not recognize him. He had long walked past me in the airport arrival lounge before my memory was awoken by that walk – that springy, vain, 'captain-of-the-soccer-team-and-still-best-in-class' walk he had always had. It was not the age that had confounded me, nor the fact that he was clad in a three-piece suit, complete with a khaki safari hat, monocle, wing-tipped shoes and a pipe. No, first and foremost, it was his face. It looked as if it had been reset – as if every feature had been taken down one by one then replaced in a hurried and haphazard fashion, so that now each was a sort of caricature of its former self. He looked oddly disassembled and incongruous. The second confounder was the peach-and-pink wispy blonde at his side. Thank goodness he spotted me first. He came forward tentatively pushing a trolley laden with a beautiful set of three enormous suitcases.

'Welcome home,' I said to them both, and thought I saw his anarchic features grimace.

He greeted me and, turning to his companion, said, 'I should like you to meet my wife, Eleanor. Darling, this is my cousin, Mrs Shungu.'

I extended my hand, saying, 'It is a pleasure to meet you. You may call me Amai Zenzele.'

'How do you do,' was the cordial reply. My hand remained suspended and Mukoma Byron shook it briefly on her behalf. The driver loaded their things into the car. As we drove through town, I played the guide, pointing out the botanical gardens, describing the climate, showing them the city centre and the different suburbs. I heard Mukoma Byron give a low whistle of astonishment as we passed through the gate and turned into our driveway.

'What a lovely home you have. Things have changed

so. I hardly recognized Salisbury as we drove through it.'
It was my turn to grimace.

'Yes. I never dreamed that Rhodesia, or any place in
Africa, would be so peaceful, lovely and clean,' chimed
in the Wisp in a misguided attempt (no doubt) to make
amends for her earlier *faux pas* in African courtesy. I
could not bear it. It was like a personal insult.

'Thank you very much. I hope that you will find our
home, *Harare* and *Zimbabwe*, as they are called now,
much to your liking.' I shot Mukoma Byron a questioning glance which he quickly avoided by stooping to
retrieve his hat. It was absolutely unforgivable for him to
address this land that we had struggled so long to call our
own by its colonial name! To outsiders, perhaps,
Zimbabwe is just a name signifying some random
geographical boundaries. It is a noun like mango, pen or
car. But for me it is different. Rhodesia was a forbidden
country for me, a white man's playland. There were vast
homes, pristine schools, safari parks and city clubs, but
because of my colour, I was not permitted to enter there.
I was always outside looking in, yearning and wondering, What does that feel like? What does that taste like?
And I did not know until years of bloodshed and turmoil
later, just how sweet life could be here. Who could have
known there was milk and honey for the taking, right
here in my own country! I shall never forget the day I
stood on the pavement in town, transfixed, as they took
the dreadful, prohibiting letters spelling Rhodesia down
from City Hall and put up, one by one, the name that
gave me the keys to the kingdom of my country. I had
inhabited Rhodesia, but in Zimbabwe, I lived. You are
too young to bear the scars of years of exclusion and so
you cannot see that each letter of that precious name
holds a promise. It assures me that by law I can enter any

shop, any office, any hotel, any restaurant; that I can walk with my head high if I please; it says that I can enjoy like any other the beauty of its fields and rivers and above all that I can possess a piece of this land for myself and my children. Oh, for me this is quite enough to make me puff up with pride, but just ask your father if you want the full patriotic version. To him Zimbabwe is like a horizon, boundless in possibilities. I am not political, as you are painfully aware (this is a source of disappointment, I know), so I cannot truly call myself a nationalist. Yet, for all my nonpartisan, pacifist inclinations, it irks me no end to hear others disregard the thousands of lives laid down, not to mention the untold sufferings of young fighters and old village folk that gave us these very freedoms. I could not believe Mukoma Byron, who, mind you, in his day was quite vociferous and opinionated about things, should be so insensitive – even offensive. I suppose I should have paid greater heed to these early warning signs. He was extravagant in all things – he ate *sadza* with his knife and fork while the rest of us dug in in the traditional way, with our hands; the pipe; the exaggerated accent; his insistence on having tea exactly at ten and four. Perhaps the most telling of all were the luggage labels, in his own handwriting, which I recognized still after all these years, written 'Mr and Mrs Byron Makon, 122 Cheshire Court, London'. He himself had dropped the terminal 'i'. I had blamed the innocent telegraphers, when the man himself had done it. I was shocked. But even then, I figured he was simply trying to impress others, as those recently returned from abroad so often do. I would never have guessed in my wildest dreams that he would go to the lengths that he ultimately did.

That evening at dinner he asked for a favour. 'I need

your help. I received a cable that my mother is desperately ill. Could you send for her for me? I simply could not put Eleanor through the strain and fatigue of the rural areas.'

I was appalled, and your father dropped his knife. We had taken a special trip to see his mother the previous weekend. The poor old lady was on her deathbed. It broke one's heart to see that proud spirit struggle to overcome the frail, thin body. Her wits were as sharp as ever. She felt disgusted and betrayed by her 'useless' body. She cherished the dream of her son, the doctor, returning to save her.

'Oh these rubbish local doctors, what do they know?' she would say, spitting out her medicine. She was a terrible patient. 'They have no idea what ails me. Let my son come and show them a thing or two. He was educated with whites in Ingrand.'

She was merciless with poor Dr Chinaka, who did his best to take care of her. 'You can do as you please now, va Chinaka, but as soon as my son comes, he will save me from your wretched clutches,' she would heckle at him.

I turned to Mukoma Byron before your father could say a word. I could tell from the single raised eyebrow and the violence in his grip of the newly retrieved knife that he was about to deliver a withering lecture to Mukoma Byron. As I spoke I saw his jaw muscles flex and his temporal muscles twitch to suppress his disdain.

'I think that would be ill-advised, Mukoma. Baba va Zenzele and I saw her a few days ago. She is quite weak. I had planned to take some sugar and flour to her and Mbuya, Baba va Zenzele's mother. As I am sure you are anxious to see her, I shall try to rearrange my schedule so that we can go tomorrow.'

Over the next twenty-four hours I schemed and

manoeuvred to have a few private words with Mukoma Byron. I was convinced that if we could just talk, all of this pretence would fall away and he would be my wonderful hero of old. I soon realized, however, that while I was seeking him, he was avoiding me. He became uncomfortable whenever Eleanor was not with him. I found it preposterous that in his own country he could not feel at home unless he was with a foreigner. He also refused to speak Shona. That infuriated your father and baffled me. If I addressed him in Shona, he would look blank and say, 'I beg your pardon?' or on occasion he would reply in English. He had left in secondary school. It was absurd. He was stiff and formal with us; he insisted on wearing full English tweed in the heat of the Zimbabwe summer. His accent was absurdly British. It was like listening to a Monty Python imitation of the British Broadcasting Corporation. There remained not a trace of the local accent in his voice. I had been mistaken – it was not only Mukoma Byron's face that had become an incongruous caricature; it was his entire being.

Eleanor did not accompany us to Chakowa. Byron feared for her comfort and warned her that he did not trust the water 'out there'. I doubt she could have caught anything even if she had sat in an infested swamp, for they had brought a full pharmacy of every antibacterial, antifungal and antiparasitic medication known to man. There were creams, powders, injections and pills of every shape, colour and size. I declined politely when Eleanor offered me some blue round pills in case I drank any unboiled water. What on earth did she think I had spent my life drinking? Champagne? It was too much. I could not understand what attracted Mukoma Byron to such a frail-looking, pallid creature. She was nervous and wore long flowery dresses that were even paler than her complexion and hung on her in a flimsy, shapeless way like clothes pinned on a line to dry. She seemed either to say too little or too much. Frankly, I was quite relieved, therefore, to learn that she was to remain in Harare. I had hoped to talk to Mukoma Byron *en route* but he feigned sleep for the entire three-hour drive.

What remained of their compound was a circular constellation of buildings: the half-bombed house of Mukoma Byron's childhood, which was all that had survived the war, the new outhouse, two chicken pens and one round hut thatched and made of the deep red clay of the region. Auntie Mai Byron raised the best chickens in Chakowa and she was a shrewd businesswoman. The chickens were a chief source of income for them. A few hardy shrubs were dotted about the yard. The rest was red dust speckled with litter.

Within minutes of our arrival, villagers began to swarm about us. Neither I nor my car drew much attention, after years of frequent visiting. It was the sight of Mukoma Byron that brought the old ladies ululating, dancing around us as we climbed up the narrow path that led from the main road to the hut. His return had been the subject of heated debates ever since his mother's condition had become grave. His family insisted that he was sure to come as soon as he received the news. Others sarcastically argued that he had forsaken his homeland, claimed English citizenship and did not concern himself with the affairs of the colonies. As the compound came into view I heard a high-pitched cry as his sister, Chipo, lunged forward and clasped him in a tight embrace.

Tears streamed down her face as she cried, 'My brother! My brother! At last you have come home. *Mwauya! Mwauya!* I knew you would not disappoint us. Our mother has longed for this day.'

With a twist and a leap she joined the league of ululating women. Her bare feet, oblivious to the stones and rubbish in the path, pounded a joyous rhythm and raised a screen of red dust before us. By the time we reached the hut, we were a full procession. At the head was Chipo, wearing a torn yellow skipper and a brightly printed *jira* wrapped around her waist in the rural fashion. Behind her followed a dusty Mukoma Byron, clad in a beige wool three-piece suit and puffing at his pipe nervously as he attempted to preserve his stiff posture despite the waves of well-wishers that surged forward to embrace him. I walked a few paces behind him. A robust chorus of village women and a pack of mangy stray dogs brought up the rear. The latter always followed a crowd. They knew it was either a funeral, a birth, a wedding or a death. Whichever way, there were sure to be plenty of scraps. Mukoma Byron looked increasingly discomfitted as we approached, but I was not certain if this stemmed from a concern over his mother or annoyance at the attention that he had drawn.

It took several minutes to adjust to the virtual darkness of the hut. A small fire in the centre of the floor and a slit window high along the far wall provided our only sources of light. On a heap of blankets along the wall opposite the door lay Amai Byron. Beside her were several enamel bowls of various sizes; some contained steaming hot water, others, herbs soaking. A stick of incense and two candles burned at the foot of her 'bed'. Chipo knelt beside her mother, whispering softly, 'Amai, Amai.' She dipped a rag into one of the bowls with steaming herbs and placed the cloth across the wrinkled old forehead. Even the mountain of bedding heaped upon the old woman could not hide the extent of her emaciation. Two thin, bony hands lay over the covers. She opened her eyes and turned to Chipo, who said breathlessly, still sweating from her dance, 'He has come, Mai. Byron has returned.'

The old woman raised one hand feebly off the covers and motioned to the darkness.

'Let my son come to me,' she said in a thin, tired voice.

Mukoma Byron still stood at the entrance of the hut. He walked slowly towards the bed. All eyes turned to him.

'You did well to return, my son,' she said in a voice that breathed a sigh of joy.

Mukoma Byron stopped a few paces from where Chipo knelt. He stood behind the head of his mother's bed. He abruptly turned to me and, addressing me in English, said, 'Please translate for me. Tell her that I can no longer speak in Shona, that it has been too long.'

I did not move from my post along the far wall for several minutes. Surely he was joking? Not speak Shona? It was his mother tongue! I was certain that he was not serious, despite his similar act in Harare. I did not think he would dare pull that stunt here. The hut was full of his relatives and old friends who looked in astonishment at him, then his mother, then at me.

'Tell her, please. Tell her that I am sorry to see her like this, that I cannot stay; however, I shall leave her as much money as she needs to see the best doctor in Harare.' I still stood transfixed and said nothing. Had he really come thousands of miles to deliver this mortifying blow to his mother? I was incredulous. He stood aloof at Chipo's side. He touched no one and looked ahead in the darkness at the fire. His mother broke the confused silence in the hut.

'Byron, is that you?' Her voice was sharper, clearer now. 'I see you yet I hear a white man.'

58

Byron turned slowly from the fire and looked straight at me. 'Shiri, I beg you.' His voice was the tired one now. I moved forward to the centre of the room. I knelt down beside Chipo and, taking the old woman's hands in mine, I began to translate that which is not said in our culture. It was difficult for me to translate, not because of his newscaster accent but because the words themselves were delivered and assembled in such an impartial manner that I knew not how to frame them into coherent and meaningful Shona sentences. I had to add respect and compassion where there was none.

'I have no need to go to any hospital or clinic. I will not budge from this bed. You shall be my doctor. Do you hear, va Chinaka? Out you go with your poking examinations and bitter pills! Dr Byron Makoni has returned. They doubted you, my son. But I never did. During all of these years their wild and wicked rumours have been more numerous and a far greater nuisance than all of the flies of the grazing fields. They have tried and tested a mother's faith in her own child. But I was strong and I prayed to God to keep you so. Ha-ha-ha! Today you have come!' She gasped for breath and Chipo began to dab her head and neck with some cool potion. The old woman raised a thin hand to wave Chipo out of the way. I looked up and even in the darkness I could see Mukoma Byron wiping his glistening face in sweeping motions and wringing his handkerchief nervously. He stuffed it in his pocket and resumed anxiously smoking his pipe. The little white puffs swirled into the blackness of the thatched roof above us.

'Please explain that I cannot stay. I have a wife and must return to England in a few days.' He sounded desperate now. The room listened in awe as I delivered this message in Shona.

'Who is this wife?' snapped Auntie Mai Byron. 'Why can she not come to pay her respects to your dying old mother?' Her eyes were closed again. She lay still. Her son moved closer towards us and bent down to whisper in my ear. 'Tell her . . .' He was shaking. 'Please tell her that I cannot take care of her because I am not a doctor, I never completed my medical studies. I could not . . . Tell her that I work in London now and have made it my home. I am sorry.' I choked on each bitter word as I passed on the dreadful confession. Amai Byron shrieked. She sat up, throwing off her covers and turned to Byron who was weaving his way through the many seated villagers towards the door. We all stepped back in astonishment at her sudden vigour. She spat at him.

'How dare you come to my deathbed and tell me such things? Have you come here to break me? For years I have awaited your glorious return. But you have come back empty handed to disgrace me! Money? Who cares for your ignorant money? What is money? We sent you overseas to learn, to drink and eat the knowledge of white men. Instead you cast away your *tsika* and learned nothing but his manners! And who is this wife who has no love for her husband's mother? She is white, isn't she? That is why you are ashamed to bring her to the place of your birth. Without me and without this village, she would not know the love that she now treasures nor the body that she holds.'

Byron was trapped. Several of the elders of our village, including Sekuru Isaac, had intercepted him as he tried to escape his mother's wrath. They formed a formidable barrier at the door. Each stood tall, shaking his head and whispering, 'You have done great wrong, my son.' He turned back towards the room. His mother was still shaking with fury.

'I am an old woman. I have seen much. But this I never thought I would live to see. You left here as my son and you return a stranger.' She spat again and raised a bony finger at him. 'I taught you Shona. Do not try that nonsense with me! You are a disgrace! Go! Leave me in peace. I pity you, my son. It is better to live and die as I was born in this poor village, with my dignity, than to wander in foreign lands, full of shame. You have robbed me of my dreams but I still have my *tsika*. Send me no more of your ignorant money; you are much poorer than I. Get out of my sight. Go! And may God forgive your foolishness even if I cannot. Mukoma Isaac, let him pass.'

The men permitted him to dart out the door. As soon as he was gone the old woman collapsed into a frail heap. She whispered, 'His days will be few and miserable.' Chipo was distraught. She soothed her and remade her bed. She touched my arm.

'Talk to him, Amai Zenzele,' she begged. I nodded a weary assent.

I took my leave of the old lady with a heavy 'Goodbye, Auntie. I shall return next weekend as usual.'

'Go well, my child,' she whispered, lying very still and keeping her gaze upward to the ceiling.

This time, no one accompanied us down the dusty path. Half an hour earlier Mukoma Byron had received the acclaim of a returning hero; now he experienced the shame of an outcast. He had fallen from prodigal son to pariah. The wrath of any elder was condemnation enough, but the weight of a mother's curse was damning. To the villagers no angel on heaven or earth could mitigate the misery that was sure to attend him for the rest of his life. They stood at safe distances at the roadside and kept their children in hand behind their skirts and trousers. No one waved as the car drove off and not one word of goodbye was uttered.

During our absence Eleanor had blossomed from pale peach to ripe tomato. Apparently she had suffered a terrible sunburn accompanied by 'dreadful' heat rashes. I wondered that any rays had penetrated at all through the layers of sunscreen and creams that lay in her armamentarium against infection and injury. Nevertheless she welcomed us back excitedly, telling us about all the 'marvellous' arts she had seen at the National Gallery.

'The sculptures were so powerful and yet so primitive!' Her eyes darted about nervously looking for approval. Had she said too much?

The next day, I steered Mukoma Byron down in our sitting room to talk. I had been up all night thinking how best I could broach the subject.

'Mukoma Byron, you are older than I. You have seen many lands and peoples that I have not. But I am afraid that your behaviour compels me to tread where normally it would not have been my place. Our old friendship and our common blood also demand that I speak.' I drew a deep breath and watched as he lit his pipe.

'This is your home. No matter what you wear, no matter how polished your speech or broad your vocabulary, you are an African. Chakowa is in your hair, the flare of your nostrils and the curves of your muscles, whether you like it or not. You cannot bury your roots; no matter how many layers of London tweed you wear, beneath is a black man. You should be proud of your roots.'

'Proud of what, Shiri? Of the mud huts? Of the children running around in rags, playing with rusted tins? Of coup after coup? Proud of potholes in the streets, queues for sugar, buses that do not work? Is that what I am to hold my head high about? Just look at Africa! The

62

only land mass populated largely by blacks and the world's most miserable excuse for a continent! There is not a single viable nation from Libya to Swaziland! They are all corrupt, poor beggars. We should be ashamed, not proud! Where are our Einsteins? Where are our Picassos? Who shall be our Churchill? Face it, Amai Zenzele, Africa is an economic wastebasket! A cultural desert and a political swamp. It is a wasteland! Absolutely pathetic!'

'How can you say such things? Have you swallowed whole every piece of Western propaganda? You sound like a parrot of their anti-African jargon. Did you sell your inquisitiveness and buy new eyes and ears with your pounds sterling? And what right have you to condemn us? You who robbed those very same villagers?' He looked perplexed. His outburst had infuriated me.

'Or have you forgotten that the very shoes that you wore were bought by the pooling of pennies by those very same villagers whom you were too civilized to touch yesterday? They gave you what they had. They believed that they were investing in a better future not only for you but for all of us in that village. You took their money, and what have you ever given back to them? Show me which finger you lifted to ensure a better Africa for our children?'

'I sent money every month,' was his meagre defence.

'Foreign cash is not the answer to our problems, my friend. Africa needs the hearts and minds of its sons and daughters to nurture it. You were our pride, Mukoma Byron. When you did not return, a whole village lost its investment. Africa is all that we have. If we do not build it, no one else will.'

'I am not a messiah. I am only one single man, Shiri. It is true that at the beginning I wanted much more. I had

63

that same dream of returning like some sort of Jesus Christ, saintly and triumphant, to save the village. It is the same trite and unattainable delusion of grandeur that every poor African who goes overseas departs with. But upon arrival, we all quickly become disillusioned.' He sank into the sofa, looking uncomfortable again. I felt that I was gaining ground at last. I continued, feeling more confident.

'Yes, you are just one, but it is the thousands like you, whom our churches and governments pour money into, who ultimately drain our resources. If our brightest minds go and never return, then it is no wonder that we have poor leadership to guide our nations, that we have no engineers to run our machinery, no doctors to staff our hospitals, no professors to fill our universities, and no teachers to educate the generations to come. How can we move forward if our future Mandelas are content to spend their days sipping cappuccinos in Covent Garden? If our potential Sembenes are happier shooting French films in Paris or our Achebes-to-be prefer to tell the stories of the Americans, is it surprising that we appear to be a cultural void? Who is left to us? You are the epitome of the brain drain, Mukoma Byron. We believed in you.' I sat back now. The victory was empty. I added under my breath, 'I believed in you.' We sat in silence for almost five minutes. Outside, beyond the open french windows, I could hear Samuel watering the garden and whistling one of his favourite tunes. The distant traffic provided a constant background hum to his songs of love. Now and again the suburban quiet was broken by the ferocious barking of our neighbour's sinister Dober-man pinschers, announcing the arrival of an unfamiliar and unfortunate guest. Mukoma Byron was the first to speak and I had to lean forward to hear him. It was the first time that I recognized a hint of the old Watt in him.

'You have not been abroad, Shiri. It is not like it is here. Home is easy and sure. There are simple rules to live by. There is a moral code to which we all ascribe. Respect your elders; follow the customs; study and do not question authority; the teacher is always correct; find a job and get married. Everyone plods along in blind faith. It is like a well-trodden path and no one has dared to explore the road less travelled, that grassy, fresh expanse yet untouched by us. I arrived in London on a rainy, foggy morning with a useless, obsolete map of the world. I was so naïve, Shiri. After the initial shock and awe I began to question everything. *Everything*. Then suddenly I could not determine the right or wrong way, the good versus the evil. It all seemed the same in the end. There were so many lies and contradictions, so many questions, and I could find no answers.' He crossed his legs but did not look at me.

'You should have come home, Mukoma Byron, if you felt lost,' I whispered, full of compassion and guilt. I remembered those tortured letters and my own inability to respond, my own helplessness in his confusion. I had failed him. I remembered how in the beginning he had wanted my response to those questions. But I was confounded by the questions themselves. I could not even begin to formulate a response. It had seemed to me then that our lot was not to find meaning but to work and eat and play. Could I really stand in judgement of him? Up until then, I had been filled with scorn. He had failed us, failed his mother, his country, his people. He was a traitor, a defector. Suddenly, I realized that I myself, as much as the Methodist church, his own weakness, even Eleanor and whatever temptations had brought him to this, was a partner, an accomplice in his process of alienation.

'Ha-ha! Come home with what? No degree? No money? Who would pay my ticket, anyway? And how could I face those villagers? Come on, Shiri.'

'Yet you could face those same villagers yesterday? You refused to speak your own mother tongue! You did not lay a hand on your own mother! She who is your very flesh and blood.' I saw him shudder visibly as if the thought repulsed him. He scanned the room anxiously, vainly in search of Eleanor.

'I am a different man now, Shiri. I am used to the English ways. Eleanor and I . . . I am English, Shiri.' That bolstered me from my chair and I now stood before him.

'Mukoma Byron, you will never, *ever* be English. Even with that costume and your white woman, you will never be accepted. It is better to be a first-class citizen in a Third World country than a second-class citizen in the Western world.' The harshness of these words evinced a twitch of the mouth, a tilt of the head, an unsteady rise of his eyebrows and a setting of the jaw. Each movement was more like an autonomous part of a puppet than the interconnected features of a man's face.

'That is my home now. It is my world. There are things there, Shiri, things that we never even dreamed of! You can live like a man, instead of an animal.' He looked earnestly at me. I could not bear the conversation any longer, so I walked to the door slowly. It was a futile battle. Mukoma Byron had a new map whose terrain was foreign to me. His scale was distorted and his frame of reference was upside down. Perhaps he was right after all – perhaps he *was* English. Maybe it is true that after years of speaking a foreign tongue, walking foreign streets and kissing foreign lips, one is reborn. They departed on the early flight to London two days later. As we drove them to the airport, I was reminded of the tragic, almost comic, contrast between this farewell and the one between Mukoma Byron and me fifteen years earlier. His mother died that same day. They received the news upon their arrival in London. At the funeral, Chipo showed me the telegram that Mukoma Byron had sent. It simply read, 'SO SORRY. MAY SHE REST IN PEACE. CHEQUE FOR FUNERAL EXPENSES SENT. REGARDS, BYRON MAKON.' Chipo laughed at the name.

'You see, Amai Zenzele, what those people do with our names? They could not even spell Makoni!'

I smiled sadly. There was no need to add any more pain to her heavy heart. Two weeks later, I received a flowery pastel-lemon thank-you card from Eleanor and Byron Makon. I have not heard from Mukoma Byron since then. But Chakowa never forgot him. He became a lesson for all of us. Even today mothers will send their children to boarding schools, university or work in the town with the parting cry, 'Return soon, my child. Remember the curse of Byron.' He is now part of the lore of the ancients. Even your father has opinions on Mukoma Byron. His theory holds that Mukoma Byron mistook the means for the ends. After the funeral of Auntie Mai Byron the men gathered around a fire, roasting their goat head and drinking beer. Several relatives had come from Harare. They entered into heated debate about 'the case of Byron', as your father calls it, as if he were one of his dossiers. Many said that they had seen it coming, that he had been confused as a youngster. Others wanted the church money returned in full. 'No, with interest!' laughed Mukoma Gideon, our second cousin, an accountant. Some mumbled that it was to be expected – after all, his father, Sekuru Baba va

Byron, had been a drunkard and a heathen; he never set foot in church.

'What happened to Byron can happen to any of our children,' Sekuru Isaac said.

'I quite agree,' added your father. 'Byron,' he said, 'is one of many of our African intellectuals missing in action. They set off as soldiers in the battle against our ignorance but find the burden too great. They become disconnected; they see themselves as solitary pioneers in a futile struggle to uplift Africa. Instead of standing their ground at the front lines, shoulder to shoulder with their fellow comrades, they fall to the rear and flirt with the enemy. The battle continues but our ranks dwindle year after year. Our army has thinned while the other side burgeons with defectors.' This brought assenting nods from the elders, their white heads bobbing in agreement. My mother put it more simply: 'Many are called and few are chosen.' That was her only comment on the matter.

If we could only learn from nature; it is our classroom. The trees bear fruit; the fruit contains the seeds; the flower bears the pollen. The earth regenerates itself; it sows, then reaps. We must develop a cultural ecosystem – some eternal cycle of African regeneration – planting our roots firmly, spreading and growing as the tubers and rhizomes, deep in the earth, and sowing in our children (the fruits) the seeds to reap another harvest. Each time one of us, like Mukoma Byron, is lost to the West, it is worse than losing a fruit, we also lose the seeds therein. For me personally, Mukoma Byron's fall was equal to that of an archangel. I had looked up to him so. For me, his departure had all the promise of the treasures of the Western world. So his return in disgrace was a refutation of that illusion. After all, Mukoma Byron had been an almost perfect seed and the Western soil was ideal, rich and nurturing. How, then, could such an experiment yield such rotten fruit? It was like a perfect recipe, full of the finest ingredients, that when prepared forms a poisonous repast. Maybe the world out there was not so great, I thought, and since then I have maintained a healthy scepticism of the benefits of a Western education. It seems to me that it comes for some, although by no means all (look at your father), at too high a personal cost. In the years that followed Mukoma Byron's visit, I have witnessed many others fall from cultural grace. Do you remember Sekuru Chivu from Paris? And Auntie Barbara in Toronto? They all succumbed to moral anarchy and glittering materialism. They returned with eccentric ways and a peculiar cultural amnesia. They became foreigners in their own land. To this day they remain disillusioned and restless, seeking that which they have long discarded and forgotten.

Yet we are also to blame as a society. We send our children into the unknown with little preparation. For four or more years they are isolated from all that is familiar: the sound of their own language, the feel of *sadza* in their hands, the wisdom of their elders, and the warmth and security of their families. They learn physics or economics; they hear of atoms and principles that have no translation in our language. The chasm between the new world and the one they have left behind grows irreconcilable. It may even erode their confidence in their people. Rather than come to terms with this dual nationality, they reject the old and embrace the new. It is little wonder, then, that after so many years, the children return as bizarre cultural mutants, comic replicas of their hosts. We glorify the Western world. It is true that we wish our children to return with diplomas, but we rejoice no less to see them laden with chests of electronic treasures – televisions, videos, cameras, stereos, cars and computers.

I realize that much of what I have said of the Western world has been negative. I do not mean to be anti-Western. Nor am I placing Africa as a helpless victim of Western imperialism. I am simply trying to share some of the pitfalls that we have experienced and seen others battle with. I would not let you go if I did not believe you had courage enough to remain true to yourself. Let these peasants, this house and this crazy clan of ours be your mirror, your foundation and your point of reference. You can arrange us as you wish – to serve as a map to guide you as you navigate your way in a foreign land. Please remember that your arrival marks the beginning, not the end, of your journey. It is a long and challenging trip. You are a sojourner there, just passing through. You will eat, study, talk and travel with friends of European and African origins. It is our hope that you will draw genuine wisdom from each encounter and each adventure. Just remember at the back of your mind that you are preparing for very different realities. Their sense of reality is the modern Western world. You, however, have dual citizenship, even global citizenship. You must absorb multiple frames of reality. Keep your eyes wide open. Take in the good and reject the bad insofar as you perceive them. Remember that your ultimate destination is the home that you left. Africa will be whatever you and others like you make of it. Without you it is nothing.

V

With the arrival of your immigration and acceptance papers came the sobering realization that you were actually going to move abroad. For weeks you plagued your father and me with questions about his postgraduate work in New York and our many trips abroad on business. 'How cold is winter there, Mama? Baba, is it true that they eat snails? Elisa said she went to France once and she had frogs' legs and snails for dinner! I'll take *sadza* and *derere* any day. Yech!' 'What are the people like, Mama?' 'How are the American blacks treated, Baba?' 'Are the students really clever?' We countered these as best we could. But we knew that unfortunately nothing we could say, nothing that you have read, seen or heard will prepare you for what you shall experience in the Western world. I know that Europeans are no novelty for you. You have attended international schools and we have a constant stream of foreign guests at home, but it will be different now. Here, you meet them in your land and they must respect your culture. There, the tables will be turned. You shall be the foreigner; it will be you with the funny accent and the odd ways – you will be judged on their terms. Unfortunately, few Europeans regard

Africans as equals. They see us in the indistinct haze of a colonialist hangover. Be prepared to meet many who still see Africa as one large amorphous mass: the Dark Continent, a primeval swamp, misty and steaming, inhabited by Neanderthal creatures and cheerful but primitive natives who engage in sordid ritualistic ceremonies, deep into the night, to the frantic rhythm of drums.

That reminds me of the story your father told you just before you left. You had been begging him for days to tell you more about his student days in New York. He finally gave in one Sunday afternoon when you had been particularly insistent.

'All right, all right. My goodness, a man can have no peace in his own house!' Your lips were pressed together, triumphant, eyes set, film rolling.

'I shall never forget, years ago when I was head of the African Students Union, an active, dedicated and eclectic body representing virtually every country from Lesotho to Mali. It was in the heyday of the black consciousness and Senghor's powerful Négritude Movement. Not one of the women would have dared plait in blond extensions or wear blue contact lenses, as we hear they do now in an effort to "pass" as white. As if pallor were a passport to the promised land of assimilation. No indeed. Black was beautiful then. Dashikis and Afros were the emblems of Afro chic. We listened to James Brown and Aretha Franklin; we read Fanon, Nkrumah, Davis, Baldwin and Angelou and wore BLACK PRIDE buttons on our faded denim jackets. Our black American brothers and sisters named their children Omaju or Kumati and joined in African potluck dinners. They held their heads high and spoke of black power. We had unity; we had vision. Now all that we read and see is of integration, assimilation and social mobility. It was a different age then.' He sighed. Slowly he leaned forward towards his captivated audience, in his element now, and continued.

'Anyway, every year in spring, the African students held a symposium on African culture, politics and development. It was a grand affair, a campus-wide event, with debates, lectures and workshops that involved every department from Literature to Political Science. On the last day the students held a dinner. We were ecstatic because the conference had been well attended, the carefully chosen speakers had been of the highest calibre from academia, and the diplomatic corps had been provocative and interesting. We had asked the new chairperson of the African Studies Department to say some concluding remarks. It was purely a political gesture; the students thought it a good idea to maintain good relations with the department. She was a grey-haired white anthropologist from California and her total cumulative experience of Africa was three months living with a family in Uganda as a graduate student ten years earlier. It was little wonder that many of us questioned the credibility of her appointment.

'After congratulating us, she said, "I just love Africa. It is so beautiful, and the people are the warmest in the world. I enjoyed your conference very much. I am disappointed that there were no drums, however, at your symposium. My husband and I, during our stay there, used to just love hearing the little village boys playing at night. I cannot imagine any exhibition, or even discussion on Africa, is complete without them."

'After she sat down, there was an embarrassed silence. The insult would have been of little importance had we not been aware that the future of African studies there was under her leadership. Presumably there would be a flurry of research in African drums! Her comments generated more heated debate that evening than all of the seminars combined! Fifteen seething Africans squeezed into my microscopic bachelor flat on the hip Upper West Side of Manhattan afterwards. Within minutes a smoky mist hung in the air which was thick with the din of foreign tongues. I remember Madiaw Ndiaye, a towering, intensely dark and brilliant Senegalese medical student, impeccably dressed as always, was particularly irate. He stood on one of the chairs, shouting, "We must send a petition and demand her immediate resignation!" This suggestion was greeted by loud cheers. I slept not a wink that evening; we debated and argued until dawn. We denounced one neocolonialist practice after another. Some would doze off in their chairs only to awaken an hour later to plunge themselves into some fresh discussion, as impassioned as ever. In those days every one of us was a revolutionary. Any one of us could have been the next Nkrumah, the next Mandela or the next Luthuli. We raised money for our freedom fighters in Rhodesia, South Africa and South-West Africa as they were called then. We printed leaflets and marched around campus with placards. Tammi Nkosi, who was from South Africa, did a hunger strike once for two weeks to highlight the plight of the prisoners at the apartheid regime's notorious Robben Island. We were young and energetic; we believed in the new Africa to come.'

I suddenly felt all alone in my corner chair, knitting. I was outside the glow of admiration that you were beaming on your father. He was chuckling, folding his glasses and shaking his head. He took up his *Business Herald*, still chuckling and mumbling, 'Drums, drums. Dear God, the woman wanted drums.' You were fascinated – delighted to have found a fellow comrade in your own father.

'So, what happened, Baba? Did you send the petition?'

'Oh yes, we did. She naturally stayed on and we were chided by the dean's office for not having any sense of humour.'

I must admit it gave me a little satisfaction to see that you were a little disappointed by this.

'But in the end it was no matter to us what the administration officials said or did. The incident had a profound effect on all of us. We had learned a valuable lesson that evening. That little story goes beyond student activism. Its theme lies at the heart of our post-colonial dilemma. You see, Zenzele, the African students, as many of our African leaders do today, had sat down together and generated an agenda of what they thought were critical issues facing our continent. The programme was designed and executed by Africans. Clearly, the anthropologist had quite a different vision of Africa. While we were seeking to enlighten, she was in search of entertainment. She subscribed to the doctrine of wildlife first, noble savage second. Unfortunately, she was the one with the power to appoint members of faculty, direct research, allocate funds and publish books. This is exactly our predicament with the powerful countries of the North. To them, we are the Third World, the backward countries, the developing, the underprivileged world. Their agenda for us changes with each new trend in their own thinking, so that our course is never consistent. One year we must generate a middle class; the next year they want to dump us with their technology; the following year they recognize that appropriate technology is the answer; and so it goes. This year, the key is empowering civil society, whatever that means. If we export to them, we can earn their currency in order to pay off the interest on their loan to us and buy our raw materials back once they are processed and packaged by them! It is an absurd situation. We grow tea; they sell us the tea bags. We grow tobacco; they make the cigarettes. We grow the fruit; they sell us the jam. It is called free trade by one half of the world and "economic exploitation" by the other. They measure us by the balance of trade, the gross national product, the *per capita* income and the infant mortality rate. Our indicators of health-care equity, education for all, the family, the drug-free schools, expenditure on services for the disabled and handicapped – these have no place in their economic ledgers. Yet these reflect our values and our achievements. All I am saying, my daughter, is keep your eyes open out there, continue to ask as many questions of them as you do of us, and you will not get lost. You will make us very proud, I am sure.'

I was knitting a red cardigan for you. While I was working to weave you something warm and protective, your father was exposing you to the harshness of life. My hands could not keep pace with his words. You would one day outgrow my sweater, but his story would suit your body, mind and soul perfectly for eternity. His words would become a part of you, while my little jumper would always be external, an extra layer between you and the world outside. He would win, because you stood on common ground. Why can I not see what you see? Where are you looking? There is a vision of some 'greater-than-this' that you share but that I cannot see – some snapshot that you carry around like a soldier of his beloved, which gives you the courage to fight, to cast away this domestic tranquillity that I have created for you, and to seek out life's difficulties. I stood apart from you activists. It was as if I had skipped through some critical developmental milestone in the metamorphosis from pre-colonial clone into the post-Independence Zimbabwean. Seeing your father returning to his pile of legal documents, I was terrified that you would turn to me any second and, giving me the benefit of the doubt, ask if I had been involved in any student movements during the liberation struggle. I hastily put my wool and needles aside and escaped into my haven, the kitchen, to check on dinner.

That evening and for many weeks afterwards, I reflected a great deal on that story. I have thought of the many people I have met and things I have read on Africa in foreign magazines and journals when I was abroad. According to many, particularly the 'do-gooders' – the missionaries, the developmental organizations, the so-called experts, and the Western philanthropists and anthropologists – our continent has no life, no definition, and no spirit of its own. It is an object to be acted upon. It needs to be moulded, freed, bought, sold, aided and sabotaged, all at the whim of the benevolent and all-seeing Europeans. Africa is like a premature infant, defenceless, undernourished and underdeveloped, unable to sustain life. It needs intensive care, a plethora of complex Western technology: emergency aid, life-support systems, and constant monitoring. Its lungs are still pleural buds, not yet ready to inhale the sweet aroma of industrialism; its heart manages only a faltering and unsteady beat, insufficient to suffuse lifeblood into its people; its inner organs are too immature to digest the delicacies of civilization; its tiny, atrophic arms lack the force to defend its territory; and its infantile brain has yet to develop the synaptic circuitry to make sense of democracy, capitalism and the true meaning of independence. It is up to us to grow up and nurture ourselves. We have to define ourselves and write our own history. Your father is always repeating that famous saying, 'Until the lion learns to write, tales of hunting will always glorify the hunter.' So it is with us, too. History is simply the events as seen by a particular group, usually the ones with the mightiest pens and the most indelible ink. Certainly the dates can be objective but the events never are. All things are relative, even in science. Look at archaeology. For years, South African, English and Rhodesian scholars argued that Great Zimbabwe could not have been built by the Bantu. Instead, they proposed that it was the Phoenicians or Egyptians. Presumably, they had trekked all the way down, built the magnificent edifice, and then trekked right back up the Nile. A most improbable story, born of disbelief in the ancient Shona capacity in architecture, metallurgy and social organization. Do not be fooled by the whitewashed apparent objectivity of the ivory tower. Until the ivory turns to a rainbow with all countries represented, you would do well to be suspicious of the so-called 'facts'. 'History,' your father says, 'is determined by its authors just as the building is defined by its architect, not its inhabitants.' Until we begin to put our pen to paper, we historically do not exist. Had we not the accounts of Livingstone, Rhodes and countless other 'explorers', the tales of Mzilikazi, Monomatapa and Shaka, our great kings and generals, would have died with the breath of our elders. Even what little information we do have is filtered through the senses of sixteenth- to nineteenth-century British and Portuguese travellers. Hardly impartial observers. What, then, of the countless other kings, explorers and warriors who never encountered a European? We shall never know. Ours is an oral tradition and each time one of those ancients dies, we lose an entire century of our history. We cannot continue like this.

I confess that I leafed through your little red university prospectus/Bible. There was an interesting course entitled 'Western Art from the beginning to the present'. I saw from the description that it was one of those typical sweeping and superficial undergraduate survey courses, common among universities. To my great astonishment, it began with an extensive section on Egyptian Art! The West has appropriated the richest store of African art and civilization. The gigantic museum-palaces of the West spawn room after room full of our most bizarre masks, our most elaborate jewellery, our most majestic statues of Egyptian kings and queens, our pottery, and even our graves. You will see the heads of our beautiful Queen Nefertiti, who, with a few touches of preservation, retains only traces of her African features: her skin is lighter; her nose is straighter. No matter, my dear Zenzele. Own your history. As your father says each time he folds up the *Herald* or listens to the news, 'The scramble for Africa may be over, but the struggle for her history, her art, her literature and her children rages on unabated.'

VI

You are a rare bird, Zenzele. You shall be distinguished overseas by your colourful plumage, graceful flight and beautiful songs. There are so many lovely features that will make you conspicuous among the flock. One of these is your colour. In our country you are accustomed to every shade from caramel to charcoal. Overseas, they do not have an eye for our rainbow. To them, we are all one burdensome colour: black. It would be deceptive and negligent if I did not prepare you for the meaning of being an African abroad; if I did not warn you of the implications this has for every aspect of your life, from the subtlest nuance to the most overt hostile reactions. It is, first of all, automatically to be in the minority. Think of our descendants in the Americas, Europe and Asia. The land is not theirs; the governments, the banks, the universities – all are run, owned and populated by the majority. By definition, our views can be cast aside by the mainstream. You are outnumbered. Your place in society is virtually defined by your lack of power. Being black sometimes means waiting an extra five minutes in the queue, being ignored and dismissed by the saleslady in the clothes shop because she does not believe you are going to buy anything. It means tolerating long, rude stares in distant cities like Madrid and Warsaw. Did I ever tell you about the visit your father and I made to Warsaw? He had been invited to speak at a human rights' summit. It was a grand event, with all the major lobbying and government heads. We arrived a day early to visit the city. We had not meant to cause such a commotion. Children tugged at their parents' arms as they trailed behind, their little eyes bulging in disbelief, mouths wide open in astonishment; even the adults would lean out of their cars to get a better look at us. In fact, in the old square, we nearly caused a head-on collision between two drivers who were distracted to carelessness at the simple sight of us crossing the road hand in hand. People were so very curious yet so very fearful, as one often is of the unfamiliar. It became quite amusing after some time.

One afternoon during the conference, I set out on my own, as I had had enough of glorious speeches and generous pledges to the rights of all mankind. I had spotted a quiet café in a charming cobblestone corner of the Old City. I was served last and greeted by many questioning eyes as I began to sip my tea. To my surprise, an old lady, whom I remembered passing several blocks back, suddenly sat herself across from me without so much as an 'Excuse me' or a 'How do you do?' I found this quite rude. She ordered a cup of espresso, from whose steaming brim she observed me with a persistent, unabashed stare. Thankfully, I had brought along a thick book to read. I buried my head in it, hoping that she would take the hint.

'Excuse me,' she said in a thick Polish accent. I looked up expectantly and gave a cautious smile. Poor little old lady, perhaps she was one of those café bag ladies found in the urban chic of Europe, or perhaps she was just a lonely old bird. I know how often the aged overseas are estranged from their families. She was dishevelled and had a face that hung to her bony structures with little tenacity, so that it slipped and sagged around the chin and cheeks. She had a small tuft of grey hair that sat like a mound on her chin and the grey hair on her head was tousled in all directions. I pitied her instantly.

'You new in Poland?' she ventured.

'Yes. I have just arrived,' I said.

'Where you staying now?' She leaned forward.

'Nearby. Not far,' I said, being deliberately vague. I had heard of the notorious gypsies of Eastern Europe who robbed unsuspecting tourists.

'You can cook?' asked the old lady in a hoarse whisper. Her face was so close to mine that I had to catch my breath not to inhale the odour of her thickly coated tongue and scraggly brown teeth. I was startled by this. Yet she looked even more earnest. 'You need work? I have small house needs good cleaning. I have two grandchildren, very nice. No trouble for you. You can live with us. I feed you.'

I nearly dropped my book, I was so mortified. All I could do was stare disbelievingly into her expectant eyes. I was dressed casually, befitting a day for walks and visits to the local museums, but I certainly did not look unemployed or homeless. And really, what would a poor recent immigrant be doing in a café reading and sipping tea? And for that matter, there wasn't even any milk available in the place! No matter how bad it got in Zimbabwe or Rhodesia in drought, war or economic isolation, through financial upheavals and international sanctions, one could always get a proper cup of tea in the afternoon. When I told your father the story that evening

82

in our hotel room, he howled with laughter.

'Ha-ha! Oh, that's a good one,' he said, wiping the tears of mirth that were streaming down his face. 'So, did you take the job?' This set him to laughing all the more. I was not in the least amused. I turned away so that he could not see my hurt, but he caught my hand and gently squeezed it.

'Amai Zenzele, sit here, my dear. In my travels I have been mistaken for anything from a janitor while innocently standing waiting for the lift in a bank, to a bellboy of the hotel while waiting to collect my keys at the desk. At the reception desk someone will invariably drop their luggage at my feet and say, "To room 506, please," then fish for a tip in his pocket; or, while I am walking to my table in a restaurant, a hand will reach out to grab me and impatiently ask me for the menu; and I cannot even count how many times, while leaving a friend's flat at night, I have been harassed by the security guards as if I were some thug. Five years ago, I went to Frankfurt to visit our old neighbour, Mathias Holtzman. He had returned to his native home after some twenty years in Zimbabwe. As I was leaving the building, his doorman barred me from exiting and insisted on searching me from head to toe. I even had to show him my passport and visa! Having found nothing on my person or among my documents to confirm his suspicions, whatever they were (I simply presumed they were the usual), he had the audacity to call up to Mathias's flat and make him come down and testify that he knew me and that I was a respectable human being! It was mortifying for both of us. Then and only then did he let me loose on his precious city. Poor Mathias kept apologizing. Even to this day he blushes whenever I see him. For in Zimbabwe, he was treated with great civility. These little incidents, these sharp reminders that all are not equal in the sight of man, occur irrespective of whether I am wearing a three-piece-suit and carrying a briefcase, or merely wearing shorts. Welcome, my dear, to the Western world, land of democracy, freedom and bigotry. Don't ever think that racism was a fleeting, isolated virus to which only the Rhodesians were susceptible. Oh no – unfortunately, the entire world is infested with the malady. No one, black, white, Indian or Asian is immune. But what happened to you today had nothing to do with you as such, Shiri.

'Prejudice is in the eye of the beholder,' he said solemnly, still holding my hand. 'Racism is a phenomenal thing; it is like a thick mist that obscures the vision and judgement of even great minds. As far as that lady was concerned, you are black, and that means you are automatically poor and in need of a job. To her, you are neither short nor tall, neither funny nor dull, nor fat or thin, nor pretty (wink) or ugly. To her colour-blinded mind's eye, your three dimensions are black-by-black-by-black. She could have no way of knowing that you have your own full staff of servants at home. In fact, if you told her, she would not believe you anyway. It is beyond her realm of experience. You are beyond her microsphere of credibility. It is like Rhodesia all over again. The rest of the world got stuck in the Smith era of apartheid while we moved on.'

'But Baba va Zenzele, I was dressed normally. I was reading a book in a café, for heaven's sake!' I got up and waved my arms about in frustration to make him understand the absolute absurdity of the scene. 'What on earth did I do to make her think that I was a maid? To think that I could ever work for such a filthy woman or anyone in that capacity. I felt so insulted, so cheap, even dirty, somehow.'

'But Amai Zenzele, don't you understand? That is precisely my point. They don't see you. One cannot take racism personally. If you begin to doubt yourself, then the battle is lost. It has nothing to do with your voice, your looks, your charm, your intelligence, your attitude, and certainly not your achievements. It focuses on one thing, one variable only, to the exclusion of all others – your colour. To question yourself because someone treated you like a second-class citizen is like judging your self-image by the reflection you see in those circus mirrors that stretch your face out wide and pull your torso to your toes. They have such a distorted image of who you are and what you are. The true reflection of you lies within. The internal mirror will never lie.'

I have come to understand this with increasing clarity over the years. It is their ignorance of us that causes them to treat us so. But it is a bitter pill. I know how tough it is to hold one's head up high in the train, the metro or the bus when the seat next to yours is the last to fill up and people prefer to stand rather than sit next to the black, and you look straight ahead, pretending not to notice, and repeat to yourself, I do not smell; I am not dishevelled; there is nothing wrong with me. It is them. But it is just so. I owe an Italian countess for proving this to me once and for all.

Do you remember two years ago when we flew to Geneva so that your father could accept the Blue Diamond Award for his work on political prisoners during the liberation struggle? At the evening reception, my attention was captivated by the entrance of a stunning young woman. She was fantastically dressed in a sparkling, sequined gown of the most gay lime, azure and fuchsia. The dress was so well fitted to her slender form that she had the appearance of a mermaid floating through the crowd as it swirled and foamed about her ankles. She coquettishly accepted a drink from one gentleman and a light from another. I watched as she tipped her head at just the perfect angle to catch her profile at its best, being careful to curl the smoke from her cigarette in elegant whorls to the ceiling. The soothing way she held one's hand and squeezed gently, the soft manner in which she placed her hands on one's shoulders, and the ease of her compliments distinguished her instantly as a professional socialite. Over the years, during our many trips abroad, I have learned to spot them immediately. They are well-preserved ladies, costumed in the latest creations from famous designers in Milan and Paris. Virtually every charity function and museum opening is studded with the like. Their calendars are packed for months in advance with luncheons, fashion shows and black-tie dinners. In between they squeeze in a face lift, a manicure and a visit to their favourite astrologer or psychic. They make every evening gay with their lighthearted remarks and frivolous comments. They are a hostess's guarantee that no serious or controversial discussion will occur. I have never ceased to marvel at their deft manoeuvres to attract the attention of the most prominent public figures and key political people in a crowd. I watched the mermaid out of the corner of my eye as she whirled towards our end of the room. She stopped to greet Lord Quentin with a little laugh, saying, 'Oh, Lord Quentin, I had no idea you would be here. Last I heard, you had been out fishing in Mongolia! How is your lovely wife?' She then proceeded to draw in several others in a conversation that ranged from antique automobiles to the Masai of Kenya. I was in awe. She was a true professional!

She soon moved on and engaged the pudgy French

Ambassador, Monsieur Le Roque de Tocqueville, in an apparently hilarious repartee regarding the latest minimalist exhibit at the Louvre. For my part, I milled about the room, chatting to amateur socialites like myself who darted from one familiar cluster of faces to another. We welcomed the hors d'oeuvres with a grateful smile, for they kept one's hands and mouth occupied simultaneously, obviating the need to strike a pose or feign an expression of intense interest in a conversation that one could barely hear above the din. No, for us it was enough to nod at the appropriate intervals in discussions and smile distantly. Your father, however, moved through the crowd with ease, accepting congratulations and challenging various views. He certainly had all the grace and confidence of a professional socialite but he could never assume the requisite flippancy.

I was quite relieved when we finally sat down to dinner, for that gave me a fixed place, a secure position relative to everyone else – my very own spot. To my great amusement I was seated next to the mermaid, who turned out to be the Countess Isabella di Cappellini, daughter of one of Italy's most revered noble families. She could trace her roots back to the emperor Claudius. For her part, she was initially haughty, no doubt most dismayed to have been coupled with such an obvious amateur, but upon realizing that I was the guest of honour's wife, and being the absolute professional that she was, she set her social expertise to work.

'Oh! You are from Zimbabwe. How marvellous!' she said with great conviction.

I smiled brightly, already reprimanding myself for having been perhaps too quick to judge her. 'Oh, have you been there?'

'Why no. But I have heard that Africa has the most glorious wildlife and I hear that in your country there is a grand waterfall.'

'Yes, Victoria Falls. It is a beautiful country. It appears in summer a little like the country outside Rome,' I said trying to make the landscape imaginable for her.

At this she seemed genuinely startled and raised her eyebrows.

'Oh, you have seen something of Italy?' Those were her actual words, but I swear what she really meant by her condescending tone was, 'Oh, you presume to know something of my country?'

'Just a little bit. I have been to Rome and Milan only, years ago.' We then spoke of the great sights and architecture and the history of the ancient cities. You know that I have a weakness for the nineteenth-century Italian author Giuseppe di Lotti and his epic tragedies set near Rome. I confessed this to her in the course of our conversation. I believe it was the last straw for the poor woman. She faltered in her speech; she appeared at a loss as to what to say next. I figured that this must be a singularly distressing state of affairs for a professional socialite. So I thought the safest thing would be to discuss topics that were familiar to her. In an effort to diffuse her discomfort, I brought up a few superb operas that we had seen during our last visit and then a few put on by a visiting company in Harare last year. Unfortunately, this achieved quite the opposite effect. She was flabbergasted.

'But however have you heard of such things?' she burst out at last.

As if there were no libraries, no theatres, no records, no mingling of peoples. There are so many Europeans at home, the Greeks with their cluttered shops and lively music, the English with their stuffy sports clubs and tea shops, the French with their cafés and boutiques, and the Italians with their noisy restaurants, shoe shops and operas. Really, it was not difficult for us natives to have exposure to European culture. Was that not, after all, the purported high mission of colonialism, to civilize and educate (among other less worthy goals)? It was amusing that she found me so incredible. And what would have been her reaction, I wonder, had she spent five minutes with you! Or ten minutes with your father? Or fifteen minutes in Linda's company? She would have been shell-shocked. A racist can come in such pleasant attire and speak with such beguiling words that you almost forget the malevolence therein. I was remarkable to this woman not by any objective comparison with others, particularly Africans, but relative to her expectations of what an African should know (which was apparently little indeed). And even my paltry fund of European history and civilization far exceeded her understanding of our cultures. I had heard of Napoleon but she had no idea who Shaka Zulu or Lobengula were. Needless to say she was most impressed with your father's acceptance speech.

'Oh, how marvellous!' she said, clapping her hands enthusiastically as the room echoed the applause and people rose in a standing ovation. At the end of the evening and after two hours of pleasant and varied conversation she took my hand and invited me to visit her palazzo just outside Rome.

'You must meet my friends. They will be so delighted!' She squeezed my hand as if we were old friends. 'It is so rare to meet an intelligent African!' She handed me one of her calling cards which had her name engraved in beautiful majestic gold print. I took it with as much grace as I could muster and dumped it in the ashtray on our way out. An intelligent African indeed! I was no circus monkey, no new curiosity to be displayed and shown off. Poor dear, she meant well, though; it was just her paucity of experiences that had led her to be so foolish. She had paid me neither compliment nor insult by her words. You must never be flattered or dismayed by such remarks. They are testimony to an appalling ignorance of African civilization. Nothing more.

VII

Let no one define you or your country. Some will want to deify you, to treat you like a princess, while others will want to dismiss you as a peasant. Some black sisters will embrace you; others will shun you. Men, especially, will be challenged by your strength and charm. (I pity the poor fellow who falls victim to the power and charm of your personality.)

Our relationship to our displaced brothers and sisters is an odd one indeed. We Africans tend to regard them as poor cousins. Ironically, of course, blacks in the United States and England have things that we have never even dreamed of – compact little machines that with a busy hum will scrub your dishes and rinse your laundry clean. Bright, plastic contraptions to chop, whir and blend adorn their kitchens. We here still beat and wring our clothes then hang them out to air and dry in the freshness of the dawn's rays. Most English and American blacks are cared for in hospitals with beaming, uncluttered floors and well-stocked shelves, fancy computers and ultrasonic devices to detect even the smallest hint of disease. Our little clinics and crumbling hospitals have long queues, empty medicine cabinets, and are spilling over with old ladies and crying babies. And while we sputter and bump along in our 1960s cars they cruise about town in the latest models with turbo engines with cooling fans built in. Well, I could go on and on. We have none of these luxuries, to be sure, and many will be a long time coming to our part of the world.

But our pride derives not from these material things. It is just that we are close to the soil. That is where the African foundation is. We are still standing on the ground of our ancestors, we are rooted where others were scattered. We have fought off those who sought to take this native earth from us, the colonizers, the big companies, the mercenaries, even the missionaries. We have struggled and won what was truly ours. Now we must fight the enemy within. The soul of the African is deeply connected to the earth. We were the first to spring from it and our crumbled remains lie buried in many lands. Until about five years ago, I had no experience with blacks in America or Europe. I had always wondered how they could exist in foreign lands so far from their true origins. As the ancients say, the baobab tree, as majestic and solid as it is, would wilt if it was removed from the rich springs and the plentiful soil that give it life. I remember saying to your father once that it must be so very difficult to take root, to blossom and to flourish without nourishment from one's own soil. In fact, for years I took a most condescending view of the diaspora. They were as foreign to me as the lands they lived in. So that I always thought of the African-Americans as big movie stars, pop singers and tall, muscular athletes.

That was, of course, before I met Sister Africa. Needless to say that was not her true name. No mother would ever give her daughter such an appellation. No, it was a constant source of amusement to us that her given name was in fact Mary William Smith. She was an African-American born in New York and raised in Billings, Montana. She claims it is a cold, barren place without a mango tree to be found at any time of year. Nevertheless, Sister Africa (or Sekai as Linda nicknamed her, for Sister Africa is always smiling), is full of warmth and she can tell you stories that make the tears roll down your face in laughter. I am trying to recall now how that dear girl came into our lives. Oh yes, how could I forget? I first saw her with Linda at some underground meeting that, once again, my sister had tricked me into thinking was a cocktail party, as she so often did back in the early years of the struggle. Even then, Sister Africa had a certain bearing that captivated one's attention. I regarded her with great scorn, however, for I immediately classified her as one of the typical born-again Afrophiles that flock to 'the motherland' looking for some missing link in their past. They travel here and there for a few days but are soon discouraged by the heat and the lack of modern creature-comforts. They confine themselves to the constant grumbling of discontented European and American expatriates. They purchase a few colourful items of native attire, board the next jet back to their homes and then become local experts on Africa. Meanwhile, they have had little contact with the very people they sought to discover. If there is a link then let us forge a new nationhood, as your father grandly says. I heard him deliver a speech at a traditionally black university in the United States, at Sister Africa's request, in fact. He said every African-American child should spend one year in Africa living among his brothers and sisters. I liked the idea. We should get to know each other as really connected branches of the same tree, not as caricatures and stereotypes delivered by a distorted media. It was

Sister Africa who touched me and made me believe in the 'many seeds, one fruit' philosophy that she was ever expounding upon.

On that evening Sister Africa was dressed in a long traditional dress in the Ghanaian fashion, with a bright orange-and-yellow leaf motif splashed against a deep aquamarine background. It brought forth the copper tones of her lucent brown skin. She wore a matching head wrap which was incapable of curbing her writhing tangle of dreadlocks. My first thought was that she looked awfully young to be at one of Linda's regional secretariat meetings. By her petite figure and her shy eyes, I guessed that she could be no more than twenty-one. She talked in serious, quiet tones and kept close to Linda and my cousin, Tinawo. I watched her link arms in girlish fashion with them and many other women, pulling them aside and sitting down to chat, fully absorbed in the moment, from time to time throwing her head back and letting out a gush of torrential laughter that would halt suddenly and self-consciously.

She did not seem to notice the many eyes that followed her graceful movements through the room. There was something charming, fresh and open about the girl. And so it happened that, despite myself, by the time they reached my corner of the room and Linda stepped forth to introduce us, I was genuinely interested in meeting her. Besides her own appeal, the fact that she was being introduced to me by Linda also set her apart. My younger sister tolerated foreigners poorly. She had the natural mistrust of the colonized towards outsiders. We had paid a dear price for our hospitality to Cecil Rhodes who unabashedly named our entire country after himself! Your auntie Linda's entire life has been dedicated to reversing the conditions that his arrival spawned. She therefore turned a keen, suspicious eye on all foreigners. In addition, Linda selected very carefully which friends she introduced me to and which she kept in her private and professional lives. I later realized it was probably for my own good and a matter of national security in those early years of the revolution, for I remained truly ignorant of the names and details of her fellow comrades. I decided that this young American must be exceptional for Linda to want us to be acquainted.

And indeed she was. She had travelled to virtually every African country and endeared herself to many, and lent her smile and her skills to our struggles. In Mozambique she braved the Renamo rebels and South African soldiers and formed cooperatives all over the eastern shore. We had to bail her out of jail in South Africa five times last year alone for various charges and misdemeanours that ranged from joining striking miners to defying her ban on public speaking. And Tinawo could bore you for hours recounting Sekai's contributions to our own battle for independence. I think she understands better than the rest of us that we are at heart one family, for she has had to learn the hard way. She always tells me how she wishes more Americans would come 'home'. She is in the tradition of Du Bois and other African-American visionaries who drifted to the continent. She was here yesterday, actually, on her way to Senegal where she is giving a poetry reading to her elite circle of African intellectuals. They call themselves the *Société de Négritude*. I think they are planning a resurgence of Senghor's movement. But that night, as she extended her hand in a warm, deferential manner, she was just a girl. She had not yet blossomed into the confident, defiant public orator that she is today. No, that night she was just a pretty American with a fantastic story.

It turns out that Mary William Smith was born to a Nigerian father and an American mother in New York City. The unlikely couple had met while her father was a law student at Columbia University and her mother was studying literature as an undergraduate there. Mary was the product of their brief and passionate liaison. They lived together for a time, and I believe her father had even started to settle down in a prestigious law firm, where he planned to stay. But then there came the wave of nationalism that swept through West Africa. Young, articulate and well-educated Africans, Americans, Guyanians, West Indians and even South Americans were meeting to form congresses and unions. Nkrumah and others were extinguishing the darkness of the imperialist era on the continent. There was a new force in the world as Africa came of age. Her father became restless. He felt superfluous in the United States. Whatever she says of him as a husband and father, which is little and bitter, to this day Sister Africa's mother praises him as a revolutionary and idealist.

Sister Africa was really just a baby when her father left them to immerse himself in the new politics of the continent. I was very touched by the way in which she told me her story.

'Oh! First there was that laughter,' Sister Africa said. 'I cannot describe it. It was deep yet gay, and very open. It was like a song, and whenever I heard it, I would raise my arms and soon I was engulfed by the laughter. Then it would be warm and full of kisses – laughter that made me twirl in the air and turn on my head; it was laughter that was soft and smooth but sometimes rough and bristly when I buried my face in it. I remember his laughter as actually having texture. It had feeling and shape and strength to lift me from my crib and high into the air. Isn't that funny?'

She smiled wistfully and nestled into the couch. We had left the party ages ago and Linda had performed some deft social manoeuvring so that without my ever really understanding how it all came about, Sister Africa was to be my houseguest for the next week. Your father was delighted, for he had heard much about her from Linda and Tinawo. We were up in the guest room, which soon came to be dubbed 'Sister Africa's room' in years to come, for she was our most frequent visitor. Sometimes she only came to shower and change between flights, and on other occasions she stayed for months, writing and reading. We never asked much of her; it was always such a pleasure to have her company. That evening we were sharing a pot of tea and continuing the conversation we had started at the so-called party. She was so trusting and open. I listened attentively, watching the shades of sadness that passed over her high brows and almond eyes.

'I missed it when one day it suddenly stopped,' she sighed. 'I remember one morning – oh, I must have been three or four years old and sitting up in my bed, waiting. I pricked up my ears, but there was no laughter. In its place was a new sound. It was high and sad. It was wet and weak and clinging. I didn't like it. It made me want to squirm and wriggle. After some time even this sound went away and then there was silence – a hard, resigned stillness. It was the silence that I grew up with and it was the silence that I could bear no longer.' They had moved to Montana for her mother to start afresh. She bore her mother's maiden name rather than that of her father, which was concealed from her. Her mother wanted to erase the past, to abolish any reminder of him.

'She never mentioned him. When I asked, she said that he was dead. But I did not believe her. We never got along, my mother and I, because we each threatened the other's identity. I wished to unearth the very past that she had so painstakingly buried. I think in a way she knew that, one day, I too would leave her. It was the logical next step after I finished high school. I worked as a waitress for a few years until I saved enough money for a plane ticket to Lagos. I had to know who he was and what mission had been so compelling that he would abandon his family. I had to be connected to something more than what I saw in Montana and across the country. There had to be more to our history than slaves and poverty and assimilation. I hurt her terribly by not going to a big, famous university and *being* something. But I tried to explain that I couldn't *be* anything if I didn't even know who I was.'

She turned to me, as if putting the question to me! That was at a time when I certainly was not sure of my own identity, other than being the lawyer's wife. I nodded slowly to encourage her.

Oh! How you remind me, now, of Sister Africa as she was then. She was in search of her own world and in the process created it. Can you believe that such a young girl arrived in that teeming Nigerian city with an old address of her father's that she had got from the law firm in New York, her passport and a few hundred dollars in traveller's cheques? It is a wonder she is alive at all and didn't end up mugged and mauled in some dirty ditch in Lagos. But that is how she is. She is a true survivor. I told her so, and she replied, 'You know, Auntie (for so she calls me), I have read that Africans all over the world are linked by slavery, but it's not true. We are linked by our resilience, that inbred evolutionary ability to live and grow and love against all odds. Can you imagine that my ancestor went to America, bound and chained in some ship, was sold, and changed hands like loose coins a thousand times? How could he have imagined that his great-granddaughter would be here, free as a sparrow, eating *sadza* and drinking tea with you? Isn't that wondrous! That is what links us, Auntie. The survival of the fittest. *Amandla!'*

By now she has become such a character. She punctuates her phrases with one revolutionary slogan or another, picked up from all over the continent. Sometimes it is *'Aluta continua'*; other times, *'Pamberi ne chimurenga'*; and when she is most passionate, she raises her hand in a fisted salute and says with meaning, *'Amandla!'* as she did now.

She had come to Africa fifteen years ago in search of her father but found instead a home. She spent her first three years in Nigeria, following every clue and pursuing the slightest trace of his existence. It seemed everyone knew of him but no one could locate him. This was partly because of his clandestine activities. He was reportedly a brilliant lawyer who had devoted himself to the cause of Pan-Africanism. He did not limit his activities to any one country, but, as Sekai learned through a long and arduous search, was as committed to the anticolonialist cause in Senegal as he was in Mozambique. She ended up getting a law degree herself in Nigeria before she moved on to Ghana, where her mysterious father was reputedly a close advisor to Nkrumah. She was adopted by a family there and she almost changed her name to Afanti. But after six months of research, she learned that he had moved on to Uganda, where he was assisting the nascent Organization of African Unity (OAU) to draft a Pan-African Constitu-

99

tion. And so it went on, for virtually ten years. She would arrive in a city, make enquiries, invariably be adopted by a family who became extremely attached to her and lent her every assistance they could. Just as she would be about to find out her father's whereabouts, he moved on. She lived with many families who took her in and taught her their ways. That is how she came to be fluent in Swahili, Shona, Wolof, Yoruba and Zulu. In the end she gave up trying to adopt the many names that people gave her. They were all beautiful but she wanted to belong to all these families and so she dubbed herself 'Sister Africa', a name she has borne with great distinction. You should hear her tell the story of how she finally caught up with her father. She is almost as good a storyteller as my cousin Tinawo and I always look forward to her visits. We sit up late at night, as you well know, in the guest room, sipping tea and chatting. It was on one such night, after her seventh release on bail from a South African prison, that she told me her most amazing encounter with the man she had spent most of her adult life hunting for.

'By the time I reached South Africa after being in Botswana for one year, I really had given up hope of ever finding him. And it was funny, because at that point it was no longer a matter of identity, as it had been all those years ago when I started my quest. I knew then who I was, for my African families had given me that. But I had heard so much about him over the years, how noble and brave he was. He was my hero. He was the quintessential African statesman, the very essence of Pan-Africanism, which I embraced with a fervour bordering on fanaticism. I yearned to meet him for the great African thinker and revolutionary that he was reputed to be.'

'But surely people knew of him there?' I asked.

'Yes, they did, but they were always suspicious. He was considered an extremely dangerous man by the apartheid regime' (that was her way of referring to South Africa) 'and indeed all colonial powers. He had massive support all over Africa and beyond. If he were ever to become a public figure to consolidate the energies of four billion people – just imagine what a formidable force it would be! That is why the people were very protective of him. So I settled down in Durban and worked at the local schools. Before long, I got myself into trouble in the usual fashion: attending funerals of fallen victims of apartheid, using the white bathrooms and refusing to call the principal *baas* when he asked me to – twice. Ooh, Auntie, you should see how loud and rebellious I became. They threw me into jail, once, twice, three times, and by the sixth in three months, they sent me to Robben Island for a week. It is a fantastic place – one of the most ingenious terrorist camps in the world concealed as a disciplinary prison. It was also one of the greatest think tanks for African leaders. All the great ones were walled up there at one time or another: Mandela, Situkele, and others. I was placed in solitary confinement, but in the day I got to sit outside with some of the other prisoners. Teatime, especially, was a great time. Some of the guards sneaked us news of the outside world. The men would exchange this information for cigarettes and other prized prison commodities. We argued about the armed struggle versus the non-violent resistance methods. I said little, as I was in awe of the company I kept.

'One day, as we were out on the bench, scorching under the unwavering South African sun, some of my fellow inmates spoke excitedly in bursts among themselves. A great leader had been caught and "tried". He was charged with high treason and sentenced to life imprisonment. He was to arrive that day. Whoever he was, I gathered he was highly respected and well known, for the activity that the news of his impending visit caused was unbelievable. I felt that I was in the bustle of an organizing committee for some spectacular international conference. Little groups formed to set up daily seminars to brainstorm on issues of national and global import. A special room was being prepared; even the guards appeared familiar with his name. Although, frankly, they did not appear in the least bit pleased to be having him back. I could see that they had deployed extra security and stricter surveillance. We were sternly warned not to start any trouble while he was there. That afternoon a tall, distinguished, grey-haired man joined us in the sunny courtyard. They all called him Baba Africa or simply Baba, for "father". He was no priest, however. In fact, according to the prison guards, he was a terrorist. This automatically meant that to us he was therefore, by definition, a hero. They were terrified of him and kept him under constant supervision. They searched him incessantly, and he always surrendered in good spirits, saying bemusedly, "Don't worry, fellows, when I do escape you will certainly be the first to know. He-he."

'Others would have received a cruel blow across the face, but for him was reserved a look of hatred and fear. Apparently he had escaped on multiple previous occasions. The next three days, I looked forward to teatime with particular enthusiasm. The old man held forth each day on the importance of unity, tolerance and awareness.

'"They will try to divide us, my friends, with their well-known 'dirty tricks' tactics. Divide and conquer is their strategy. For us, unity is victory. Do not be tempted to turn against one another. Lash out your anger not on your brother but on your enemy."

'I drank in every word. In fact, it was he who taught me the true sense of Pan-Africanism.

'"If you take a seed," he said one day, "and scatter it across the lands, some will end up in marshes, some in rich fertile lands with flowing streams, others in sand, and others among the mountains and rocks. If the seed is tough, it will adapt and survive in all conditions; if it is weak, it will perish. The same seed in one country may yield a baobab but in another an oak. Our race is a potent seed. Whether you are from Ghana or Guyana, you are born of the same seed and you will be of the same fruit. We must recognize our fruition in London, in Paris, in Dakar, in Harare and in Maputo. Our roots are deep and wide. We must extend our hearts and minds, like bridges, over the swamps of racial injustice, to link us together."

'I will never forget that analogy. The next day he got down to the nitty-gritty about the planned OAU constitution, the logistics of terms of trade and military cooperation in a Pan-African state. I was ecstatic. The prison sentence was like a political science fellowship. I had never received so much education. On my last day on Robben Island, as we were being transferred along with your cousin Keki Thahane to a jail in Cape Town, he spoke to me: "Daughter, how came you to be here?" He addressed all of us younger folk as son and daughter. It was touching, as he sincerely embraced us not only as one nation but also one family. It made my heart swell with pride that such a great man had taken notice of me. There were not many women on the island and I had shyly participated in the discussions at tea. I told him of my involvements so far and he placed a large, strong hand on my shoulder and said, "I have heard of your bravery. Keep up the struggle for a united, prosperous Africa; it is a dream worth fighting for. Your love of freedom makes you a true daughter of Africa."

'I could only stare at the gravel around my feet, searching desperately in my heart for some expression of my admiration and gratitude. I felt uplifted just to stand at his side. His face shone with wisdom, and I eventually gave up the struggle to say anything meaningful, basking instead in the brief attention of one so great. I managed to release my heavy tongue to whisper, "Yes, Baba. *Aluta continua*."

'He seemed well pleased with this. "Go well," he said, giving my shoulder a firm squeeze and looking me right in the eye.

'I mentioned that little conversation to Keki a few hours later on the bus *en route* to Cape Town.

'"Oh, yes. He asked me about you and I told him you were from America originally. He was very impressed that you had given so much to the struggle."

'"Really, Keki, you must have exaggerated greatly for him to take any notice of me."

'"Oh, no, Sister Africa. He is fond of Americans. He is a Nigerian, you know, but he went to one of those big, rich, famous American universities when he was young. Columbia, I think. Yes, he studied law there. There is a rumour that he was once married to an American woman – or was she Oriental? I cannot remember. He dropped everything for the struggle. They say he has travelled all over the continent. He even advised Nkrumah."

'I caught my breath as if I had been stabbed. All that searching, that gnawing orphanlike angst of over a decade! How tragic not to have realized, not to have burst with ecstatic recognition when the moment finally came! I turned to look back, but the road was a mist of grey dirt. In any case, we had left the prison long ago. I felt a sharp pain that seared through my heart and set my head throbbing. I let out a sob and then a cry that made the guard cast us a glowering look.

"'Shut up! No more talking, you two."

'Keki raised an eyebrow questioningly. I pretended to cough, as if something had caught in my throat. But it was my heart that felt a constrictive, choking heaviness. Keki nodded, went back to reading his paper, and we travelled on in silence. I silently sobbed the entire three-hundred-mile journey. How bittersweet that ride was. As we drove through the veld, I kept my secret and grieved, mute of voice but full of expression in my heart, my head, my entire being. I was joyous that I had found him at last. My father was Baba Africa. It was no coincidence, then. Perhaps the political mischief I got myself into was simply my genetic predisposition! In the end, I could not help laughing aloud. My mind was light with wonder yet very heavy with the burden of the truth. He would never know. Or did he? Had he meant to call me daughter? I had to let him know, but what would be his reaction? Would he welcome his bastard daughter, whom he had abandoned? He was a man who embraced the whole race as his family. Like me, he had no need of the nuclear family. I decided to work tirelessly for our common goal and to try to meet him whenever I could, but I also decided that I would never disclose my secret. I did not want to distract him with any burdensome paternal attachment. It was enough to have found him. How proud I was! It gave me the strength to keep fighting because I knew somewhere he was out there, in prison, in a basement, or on a mountain top, preaching the same gospel of Pan-Africanism, telling others about the fruit and the seeds. It almost makes one believe in predestination. And how I chuckled to think that I had literally and proverbially followed in my father's foot-steps. I kept the name Sister Africa with an even greater passion because it not only meant that I belonged to my homeland but it also ironically identified me as my father's daughter.'

Imagine that to this day she has never told him. We have urged her so often. Their paths are forever crossing (he escaped from Robben Island during a field trip the day after she left), and the irony is that she has no greater admirer than Baba Africa. He has been here on several occasions. Once, they were even here for dinner together, and he did not cease from singing her praises from appetizer through dessert and coffee. It would give the old man such joy to know that his dream of a thriving, unified Africa would live on in the vivacious speeches and passionate political heart of his very own daughter, his very own seed, that which has borne such sweet fruit.

VIII

To love is a beautiful, mysterious event; do not miss it. Be neither too cautious nor too absorbed. Too many of us reason with our hearts and experience with our heads. It cannot be so. The heart knows no logic beyond need and desire; the head has no senses except the common and the pragmatic. Neither, frankly, is particularly useful in love, anyway. Rely on your sixth sense, that little voice within. There is no preparation or protection from the joy and pain of relationships. They are inseparable twins. One follows another. And make no mistake: love is not gay abandon; it is to be courageous, to take risks and to be disciplined.

My father once took me aside as a young girl. I had returned from the fields alone. Mother had gone to take Mbuya Lizzie (her mother) some fresh beans from our garden. That morning, I had skipped school for the first time in my life. I had fallen in love, or so I thought, with a young fellow who had persuaded me to go and climb the *kopjes* near Thirty Miles Point instead of learning about Livingstone and Rhodes. I have no idea to this day if my father knew of my deviant behaviour or not. He was a man who saw much and said little. Like my mother, he believed that one's deeds were more powerful than idle words. As I mounted the steps, I saw him sitting on the porch in his rickety old chair. The centre sagged and one of the arms was broken, but still he would drag it out of the living room every day after work so he could sit on the veranda and smoke a cigarette as he watched the sun set. There was a splendid view of the river and the valley sheltered by a ring of mountains. I was absolutely terrified that he had found out. But it was too late to run now, so I mounted the remaining steps with dread.

'Good evening, Baba,' I said.

'My daughter, sit here a moment.' Whenever he spoke in that tone, that low, calm voice, he sounded like a cross between a priest giving a blessing and a judge meting out a sentence. He became omniscient and fearsome. I kneeled down on the cool floor of the veranda beside the unsteady chair. In those days you never sat in a chair in the presence of your elders, particularly not when you were in trouble. I bent my head low and awaited my sentence. I focused on the scurrying black ants climbing from the floor up the low side wall, whose bodies gleamed ochre and crimson in the glow of the setting sun. I could hear the *cling, cling* of the cattle bells echoing in the dusk as Mukoma Eddie led his herd along the adjacent path.

'There is a story I would like to tell you. Are you listening, my child?'

'Yes, Baba,' I whispered, not daring to look up. My head was already feeling heavy from shame. He told me a story that I shall never forget.

'In a quiet village near the Chimanimani mountains lived a happy couple with their baby. The husband was much older, but he was kind, faithful and gentle to his young wife. Over the years, however, the wife became restless and one day she fell in love with a young man from the neighbouring village. After several months, the lover grew weary of their secret meetings. He begged her to marry him and leave her husband. Initially, she protested, but he wore down her resistance.

'One day he said, "Darling, I need you. Let us run away together. I love you and cannot bear to share you with another man any longer."

'"But what of my husband? My child?" she protested.

'"Let us poison your husband; after all, he is old. No one will suspect us. Then we shall run away to a beautiful paradise where we can begin a new life together."

'The young woman cried and wrung her hands. "I cannot. He has been a good and honest husband."

'"Then you do not love me!" raged her lover.

'The young woman pleaded with him but he ignored her. "Since you do not love me, I am going away."

'The young woman grew desperate and in the end conceded to his plan. Two days later, they poisoned the gentle old man. They stole away that evening. They walked through dense forests and hot deserts. Every now and again, they had to stop so that she could nurse the baby which she carried on her back. Finally at daybreak, they arrived at a large river.

'"There, my darling, do you see? Right across this river and over that hill lies the paradise that I promised you. We shall be happy there."

'It was a deep and swirling river, so they waded slowly along, hand in hand, as they braved the rough waves. About halfway across the baby began to wail. The lover turned to her and said, "The child has worn you out. It is a burden to travel with and will only slow us down later. Let us start a truly fresh beginning. Why don't you drown the baby in the stream? We cannot support it any more."

'The woman was horrified. She began to sob and wail.

'"I cannot! It is my child, my very own blood." She clasped the child to her breast.

'"Then you do not believe that we shall have another family and be happy? You do not trust me? After we have come so far, do you doubt me now?"

'The woman wept bitterly as she plunged the screaming child into the swirling current of the river. As soon as the little body was swept away by the foaming waves the man turned to the woman and looked at her in disbelief.

'"There," she said. "I have done it for you. Let us go in haste. I cannot bear to stand here and think of my deeds a second longer. Let us start afresh." She was amazed to find that her lover did not stir, but was staring at her in disgust.

'"What sort of an unnatural woman are you? What sort of mother would drown her own child with her bare hands? You have killed that to which you gave life."

'"But I did it for you!" she whispered, bewildered. "Please, let us go now."

'"I will go nowhere with you! You are a murderer. You poisoned your own husband, a kind and gentle man. Now you have killed your own child. What guarantee do I have that, upon reaching the paradise ahead, after a few years you will not open your ears to another lover's charm and poison me? What if a fairer lover tempts you again? Begone, you unnatural wretch! I am going to find a wife who is honourable and true!"

'And off he went. The woman howled and pulled out her hair. She was left abandoned, degraded and alone.'

When he had finished, I gave a shudder. My father concluded by saying very solemnly, 'My daughter, you will meet many men in life. Allow none to tempt you to abandon your principles. Follow what is right. Stick to the path of honesty and integrity. You are a strong girl, let no one break you. There is not a man in the world who is worth your dignity. Do not confuse self-sacrifice with love. You may go now, Shiri. Keep these words.'

'Yes, Baba.' I scrambled up and ran to the kitchen, thanking God all the way for sparing me the disgrace of having to confess my deviance to my father. I never saw the young man again. No one ever mentioned my truancy. I had learned my lesson. I have thought of this tragic tale over and over. It has served me well in times of confusion and weakness in all things. I now pass it on to you. Remember it well.

Once, when you were five and had finished your first week at nursery, you announced that you had a 'new' boyfriend, to the great amusement of your father.

'Oh, really,' he said, 'that was quick. What happened to the old one?'

'Yesterday he wouldn't let me go first on the swings, so I told him he wasn't my friend any more.'

'I see,' he said. I could see that he was shaking with laughter. 'Let's hope your second boyfriend treats you better!'

You continued unabashed to set out the tea party for your bear and dolls. A few minutes later you looked at him quizzically and asked, 'Baba, are you Mama's first boyfriend?' This he enjoyed even more. I could not restrain my own lips from stretching and bending into an embarrassed grin.

'Honestly, Zenzele, the things you come up with!' Later your father and I would be upstairs rolling in our bed, in tears of laughter and amazement at the bomb that those little lips dropped.

As you grew older such questions became more

numerous and pointed. 'Mama, where did you meet Baba?' 'Mama, how long have you and Baba been married?' 'Mama, what is it like to see the same person every single, solitary day?' 'Mama, was Baba your first boyfriend?' I have managed rather effectively for years to evade your romantic curiosity. But I will share some of these memories with you. What are these little secrets to me now? They mean nothing if they cannot become the folklore of your wisdom and judgement. As you know it is not in our culture to discuss such things. I do not think my mother ever even uttered the word *love* except in church. She startled me one morning as we carried the laundry down to the river to do our washing.

'Shiri, at the end of the day, you will meet only two men in your life: one will make your hands tremble; the other will make them steady. The first will be your passion of youth, but like the blazing fires of the bush, it will soon die to glowing embers, then cool ashes. The second will enter your life quietly, like a thief in the night. He will be like the mighty trees in the forest that we do not see before us, yet they are there, strong and tall; in rain and sun, they dig their roots deep and shade us with their leaves. It is the second one whom you must marry. He will be a good husband and father to your children.'

That was all she said as we wound our way down the path and through the thicket that surrounded the river. It has taken me almost forty years to understand the wisdom of her words.

I met many young men who caused my heart to gallop and my lips to quiver. They were handsome, with smooth words and sharp suits. But there was only one for whom my hands trembled. He was my very first love. He was three years my senior and had smooth and shiny cocoa skin. Even without shoes, his thin but muscular frame towered almost one and a half feet above me. To my eyes, his every feature was perfect: his thin moustache, the wandering eyes, the beaming forehead. My parents, however, saw him differently. I cannot remember now who despised him with greater passion, my mother or my father. It was probably as much my fault as his. The more they expressed their disdain, the more determined I became to follow my heart. Those were the headiest days I have ever known. I cannot imagine any potion potent enough to produce my lightheaded gayness. I woke up each morning with a song in my heart and a tumbling grin that fell here and there at the slightest thought of him. I hummed in the fields, I sang while carrying a drum of water on my head and one pail in each hand as I struggled up our stony path from the well, and I tapped my feet to nothing at all during dinner. But it was not only inside. My outside, too, had undergone a metamorphosis. I took a sudden and acute interest in my hair (too nappy), my hips (too big), my face (too small), my feet (too large), and my teeth (too many). Not a single appendage escaped my scrutiny. I discovered things. My hands, for example, could do more than lift, knead and plant; they could caress and hold. My lips, too, had hidden more expression than words and laughter; I discovered a silent communion with another that knew no vocabulary. I was all new. For ten months, I lived my own private genesis, my very own tale of creation which knew no day of rest.

Even the dreary village seemed suffused with colour and adventure. Our daily meetings were a clandestine affair. I tolerated morning and afternoon as the necessary prelude to evening, which marked my awakening. We would meet on the back steps of the church, where the moon cast a warm glow and long shadows surrounded us. The stars seemed to wink at us, one by one, as though fellow conspirators. I would rush to finish my chores by eight so that I would be the first to arrive. Crouched against the cool white walls, my back supported by the imposing wooden door that on Sundays let in the choir and Reverend Chigare, I would wait impatiently for him. His duties and responsibilities were more numerous and arduous, as he was the eldest son of his father's compound of three wives and twelve children, so I often waited for what seemed an eternity. On some evenings when he quarrelled with his father, I often waited a full half-hour before I heard the familiar crunch of his sneakers against the dirt as he mounted the path that led to the rear alcove. As soon as I heard his approach, my hands would begin to tremble. They trembled, too, when he said my name. ('Why are you shaking, Shiri? Are you all right? Has something frightened you?') My hands would tremble while I was at home, at work in the fields, or while fetching water at the river, wherever and whenever I thought of him. In fact, after a while, everything seemed to quiver and quake. His presence unhinged something in my life; I was buoyed up and down in a torrent of emotions. It was exhilarating and unsettling. I became restless: my chores were too long and too many, money was too little and Chakowa was too small. It was this that my parents sensed. It frightened them, and their dislike of him grew exponentially in proportion to the depth of my affection for him. They knew that we met every evening and I never stayed out beyond midnight for their sake. To be sure, they suspected the worst.

There was a strict moral code in those days. Good girls

did their chores, said their prayers and went to bed early. Bad girls were worthless to their parents and stayed out until dawn, roaming the village in search of mischief. The old ladies who were the guardians of the village standards – for the men were too involved in their demise to be trusted as objective judges – were swift to condemn one to the latter category. It took only a careless sway of the hips, a defiant sparkle of the eyes or a bold, carefree laugh to be cast among the damned, the infamous girls of dubious virtue. It was whispered that 'those girls' would be lucky to garner a few chickens as a bride price. Good girls would bring wealth and repute to their families with the many herds of cattle, fields of maize and monetary benefits that their grooms bestowed as *lobola*. Hence my parents' anxiety that my pristine image would be irreparably tarnished by our evening rendezvous. Once, I returned past midnight, humming and giggling softly. I was horrified to find my father waiting for me in his rickety chair on the veranda with a thick buckled belt at the ready. It was my mother who saved me from a thorough whipping that day. She said in a resigned voice, 'It would be easier to order the sun not to rise tomorrow or forbid the rain to fall than to force her to give up this boy. It is no use to beat her, Baba va Shiri. Put away your belt. Her hide is thickened by the emotions of youth. She will not feel its sting.'

'We have tried to teach you what is right. The rest is up to you,' he said quietly, stooping to pick up his chair. They shuffled heavily back to their room, leaving me on the veranda, paralysed by a mixture of sadness for the pain I was causing them and awe at my mother's wisdom.

But I continued to see him because I knew in my heart that we did no wrong. I remembered well my father's little tale. But I was compromising no principles. To be with him was honest and to touch him was truth. Our relationship was one of kindred spirits. It was terribly innocent in many ways. We would sit for hours beneath the stained-glass windows above the door, talking and laughing, guarded by angels on either side and with the murals of the saints all around the walls keeping a watchful eye. Sometimes we would walk to the bridge and throw stones into the river and watch the way the little waves crinkled and creased the reflection of the moon. I cannot now recall the subjects we discussed. I only remember that they seemed so important then. There were stories, thoughts and emotions that were too much for one to understand. But when shared, they became funny and somehow bearable.

All day, I collected words, saved them like the precious coins Mbuya and I put away in the pantry, only to spend them all in one splurge of free expression when we met. I cringed whenever they teased me about having a boyfriend. To me, he was a part of me that I had missed, and now having found it, I felt complete for the first time. He was unlike any boy I had ever encountered in our village or in my life. I felt, therefore, that he was a rare and special gift. I felt that it was too good to be true. I was superstitious – I put salt under my pillow, I never wore red to meet him, I never pointed at him, and I never crossed over his right foot to pass over him. My parents, among other things, objected to his lifestyle. Mbuya hated the fact that he smoked and drank. I always knew when he had had a row with his father by the heavy smell of alcohol on his breath. I suppose a part of me wanted to save him in some way. He became my mission. I waged a crusade for his happiness, for relieving the burden of his family, for stopping his bouts of drinking, for persuading him to stop smoking. I began to attend church more regularly, to the astonishment of my parents. I would pray earnestly for God to take care of him, to let us grow old together, to let him always love me as he did. I found it incredible that so rare and extraordinary a soul had been raised in my very own village and had escaped my notice for almost twenty years. Yet, I could never quite trust my joy. I feared that at any moment he might be snatched from me.

He was reputed to be very clever but rather eccentric for our little village. He had finished his O-levels two years ago at the mission school near Inyanga. Since then he had returned to the village, caring for his extensive family and his father's affairs. He did attend a few A-level classes in the town nearby, whenever he had 'spare time'. He was not interested in university; he aspired to be a famous artist. Unfortunately, this was not considered a profession by traditional culture, but a hobby. People wanted engineers, doctors and lawyers. They wanted degrees and jobs. Baba warned me over and over: 'That boy has no future.'

I loved Sundays best of all because after church I would spend the afternoon at his 'workshop', which was really just another thatched hut in his father's compound. His father tolerated this 'hobby' because it brought in much-needed extra income for his little fiefdom. I would sit on a traditional stool that he had carved for me, surrounded by mahogany figures and chipped bits of stone, planks, bricks and finished carvings of every shape, and watch him at work. He was unperturbed by my presence. Once I had offered to leave him in peace but he reassured me.

'Stay, Shiri, your presence is somehow comforting. It seems to give my hands wings.' I looked down to hide the joy that I was certain would leap out from within me. I would then sit as still as I could, trying to recognize a beak – or was it a nose? – then a hand – or was it a claw? He could create an owl from a log, a face from lifeless stone. I was fascinated by his hands. In and of themselves they were quite unremarkable. The fingers were short, his palms were calloused and there was dirt under the craggy, bitten nails. But the moment they held an object, it moulded to his touch; it became what he willed – animal, man, bird or spirit. To this day, I do not know where my own soul lies, but I knew for certain that his dwelled in his hands. In that room, I found a spiritual fulfilment that has eluded me since. I, too, like the wood, the earth and the stone he collected, had been touched by him in some indescribable way.

I can still picture him sitting across from me in the alcove at the church the very last time that I saw him – talking excitedly, his cigarette waving so wildly in the darkness that it looked like a firefly. He rarely smiled. His face was always set in an enigmatic, removed look. So to see him so animated and laughing so freely as he described his dreams of the future – our future – touched my heart and made it sing. I made him happy and that revelation caused my hands to tremble so wildly that I had to wrap them around my knees and lock them together to keep them steady. He laughed at me then.

'You are like one of my sculptures, Shiri, like this stone, waiting to be born.' He tapped a cool, ragged block of granite on the floor with one sneaker.

'What do you mean? I am alive!' I shot back. I hated it when he played the worldly one. He was laughing at me, mocking my provincialism. He had seen cities like Johannesburg, where he had cousins, and Maputo, where his cousin Jimmy, a truck driver, would take him for company. Those were places that I only dreamed of. I had heard that Johannesburg was full of bright shiny cars and tall, mirror-like buildings. People swore that the city folk lived in long towers with one house stacked on top of another, so high that they almost touched the sky! One of the nurses in our village had a cousin there. Every now and again, she returned loaded with fantastic Zulu prints and whorls of beaded necklaces and headbands. In Maputo there was an ocean so blue and so deep that they used to say even the moon reflected its beauty and shone aquamarine, rather than white, over the sea. So you can imagine why, in those days, I had little interest in the rugged *kopjes* of the Zimbabwe terrain. I longed to see these celestial buildings and exotic cities.

'One day, I shall take you to Jo'burg. But first tell me, Shiri, would you marry me if I asked you?'

I was still piqued by the slight so I laughed back. 'No way! You who is always late? You would probably leave me standing at the altar!' I saw the firefly that was his cigarette tremble as his hand grew unsteady.

'Shiri, tomorrow, Mukoma Jimmy is going to Maputo for one week to take textiles. I am going with him to talk to some of the carvers there and sell some of my work. They make beautiful boxes and chests, Shiri. When I return, I shall bring you an exquisite box with something special inside. I have already fattened many cows for your father.' He brought his face up close now and, with a wink, gave me a tender kiss on the cheek.

'Hmm. Seeing is believing,' I said sceptically, now practically sitting on my hands to keep them from betraying the emotional anarchy that his words had wrought. 'It is late. My father will be looking for me.' I got up to go. He took one of my fluttering hands in his.

'Wait for me, Shiri. Let no one steal your heart while I

am gone. In one week we shall be together forever!'

He was so earnest that I could not look at him for fear of becoming totally unhinged. I did not even say a proper goodbye or goodnight as I skipped off into the darkness. I did turn once before ascending the path that led to our compound and saw his thin frame just where I had left him, waving at me. I waved back and sang all the way home. Just imagine: to be able to live with this boy of mine; to have little ones with powerful winged hands; to see him not just at night but in the day – every day! I said nothing to anyone. But all I dreamed of was white dresses and bouquets and bouquets of flowers. My hands were hopeless – I dropped the knife while cutting onions; I could not hold the match steady to light the lamp; I sewed with a crooked hand. I became utterly useless around the house and worse at the plot. By midweek, my mother was furious with my clumsiness.

'What is the matter with you? Are you ill? Can you not hold a knife?' she would shout in exasperation each time it fell clattering to the floor.

I stored up a treasure of things to tell him about: Sekuru Isaac's new wife, our class examination results (I had passed with the third highest marks), the new car that Reverend Chigare had bought (everyone wondered where he had got the money) and Amai Tawona's new hat (it looked like a bird's nest). I found the evenings unbearable, they seemed to drag on and on. On the evening he was due to return, I ran to the alcove in eager anticipation. I waited and prayed and waited until my father panicked and fetched me long after midnight. He never came. I cried all that night, thinking he had forgotten all about me; he had probably found some beautiful Mozambican artist with creative, steady hands to match his own.

In the morning, just after dawn, while I was collecting the buckets to fetch water at the stream, his youngest brother, Moses, came to tell me that he was dead. Jimmy's truck had been ambushed and blown up by a group of terrorist bandits in Mozambique, just ten miles east of the Zimbabwean border. I flung down the buckets with a shriek and a clanging of metal that set the entire village to wailing and mourning as word spread from one home to the next. The womenfolk came running from the fields, their little babies bobbing on their backs, and the old women stopped drinking their interminable morning tea and hobbled over. Hooves and chiming of cow bells grew loud as the young boys herded their cattle back to the pen and ran from hut to hut shouting, 'Come, there has been a death!' The quickest had begun to slaughter a few goats for the long wake, when there would be many mouths to feed. A crowd was already converging on the path to his family's compound. I could see my sisters rushing to join the other young women who had started gathering firewood, collecting pots, buying oil and gathering vegetables to begin cooking for the entire village.

I knew the routine well. Everyone had their role and together the village folk worked in synchronization to relieve the bereaved family of any responsibility. I had often orchestrated village funerals for others. There would soon be prayers and then the church women would wrap their *jiras* around their waists in respect for the dead, rise slowly, and begin their vigil of singing and dancing that lasted continuously until the funeral. There would be wailing and howling all night as their voices shrilled out the songs of sorrow. And the men would chime in with their bass and every heart would cry. Then the constant stream of people who had walked all night from neighbouring villages would begin. They would arrive with their blankets and some small donation of hard-earned money rolled tightly in a filthy handkerchief. The custom of 'touching hands' with someone who had lost another was even stronger then, so that by morning the village population had doubled with all those who had come to comfort. By then, the vehicles from Harare would start to arrive, along with the hired buses.

I watched with wonder as everyone bustled about me. I worked as I have never worked in my life. I did not sleep, nor did I eat for the three days that preceded his funeral. I was completely disconnected from my own family and from any other living being. I wanted only to be able to do something for him. I cooked, I scrubbed, I gave orders to the young men to buy drinks and to the younger girls to cook, and I fetched basket after basket of onions from our fields, tomatoes from Amai Byron's fields, *matikiti* from Sekuru Martin's plot, and fresh oranges from Tete Ellen's orchard. I drove to Mutare with his sisters to buy supplies; I cooked for his mother, his little brothers and sisters. I collected the donations and determined how the money was spent. It was also my duty to ration the food and determine each day's menu. I do not remember how I survived those days. I was grateful to those robust *ambuyas* who never let the singing die. Their wailing reverberated through me, and when I was overcome, I cast off my apron, wrapped my own *jira* about my hips, flung off my shoes, and joined them on the dusty lawn as they chanted out their hymns and beat their hips in a mournful sway. I was lost in a sea of rhythmic grief. My only relief was to offer my own choking voice up to the darkness, hoping that it could penetrate that barrier between life and death and reach him somehow as a song of love. And each night in the early hours, when the last embers of the fires had to be coaxed until more firewood could be collected in the morning, when the children had finally all been washed and put to sleep at a neighbour's; when the meat was cut and simmering for the next day's feast, when the house was aglow with candles and still, save for the heavy breaths of slumber, I would join them once again. When after wailing for hours my voice was hoarse and my feet scratched and bruised, I would slip away to the old church and sit in the alcove beneath the cross and between the saints of old, and wait. I sat very still so that I would not miss the sound of his sneakers crushing the dirt and stones along the path. I would gaze up to the heavens, disbelieving, defying the stars and moon (who appeared so distant and indifferent now), and begging God to be merciful. I prayed that it was a mistake. I bargained. I offered everything I had, all that I knew of value in this world. I offered all my father's land, I forsook any riches that life might bring, I promised to be so good as to put the angels to shame – anything at all, in exchange for his life.

It was only after they had lowered his beautiful oak casket into the grave, laid two concrete and metal slabs over his coffin, and covered that with ten feet of earth and cement that I realized that no matter how long I waited, he would never return. Once the funeral was over, there was nothing to keep my hands occupied and so I developed bouts of violent tremors. I was never quite the same afterwards. It is true that my hands ceased to shake so with time, but the restlessness and the emptiness never left me. Something that had just been born prematurely died inside me. For years, the pain was unbearable. His memory was not extinguished like the flame of a bushfire as my mother had predicted. It was more like those cyclical and unpredictable tropical storms that crash the shores of lonely islands; with howling winds they ravage every building, bend every tree, uproot and destroy gardens and with a stinging violence of showers and gales wreak destruction in their path. And so it was with me. Suddenly, at the river washing the clothes or on the bus riding to the market, dressing Linda in the morning or walking to school, a latch seemed to slip, an anchor let loose, a door creaked open and my whole world would quake. I was adrift, lonely and shattered again; there was nothing to grasp, no hand to hold me steady. Then just as suddenly, my sobbing and howling would subside. There was a hollow space deep within me. When it rained, the space flooded with tears: in the flash and crackle of thunder, it would reverberate with pain; and in the dry heat of December, it was a scorched and arid, barren place. Nothing filled it – except perhaps regret. I raged against God. I could not bear the sight of the church; I felt betrayed by the saints and angels and abandoned by God. I bore a silent resentment against my parents, too. I felt cheated. Above all, I felt powerless. There was absolutely nothing that I could do to bring him back. I understood then for the first time the meaning of the word hopelessness. It is funny the way that life serves as an empiric dictionary of its own. In those days my vocabulary grew to appreciate the true meaning of words that I had been ignorant of – hopelessness, grief, loss, depression, apathy, resignation – just as profoundly as days before the meaning of love and joy had been so very clear. My family watched helplessly and sadly as I withdrew from village life. I left Chakowa that year to enter the Teachers' Training College in Mutare (or Umtali, as it was known then). I met many young men who only aroused my curiosity.

Nothing stirred in me the day I met your father. He entered my life deftly, just as my mother had predicted, like a silent thief. Perhaps it will go differently with you. Either way, I hope those graceful hands will know the lightness of a tremor and the peaceful gravity that a beloved heart brings.

In those days, your father was known as a wild and revolutionary lawyer. He defended whomever he pleased, regardless of whether they could pay his minimal fees or not. Apparently he prided himself on being a man of principle. I had seen his offices, on the top floor of a dilapidated stucco colonial building, in the most squalid section of Sakubva, where chickens and cyclists battled for the dusty road and music blared from the open 'windows' of corrugated iron shacks. I guessed that he could not afford to rent his own place in the nice quarter of town reserved for Africans where other doctors, lawyers and businessmen lived. It was called Gloucester Court and comprised four blocks of neat, identical houses, row after row, with a square patch of grass at the front and a shopping centre and service station nearby. As it turned out, the whites had offered him a nice job as a legal clerk in a firm in Mutare, with regular pay and a little house with running water and a garden, but he refused. I'd heard claims that your father spat at the offer and vowed never to be their 'cookboy lawyer'. I met him at a party that Linda, who was now grown up and living among the fast set of rebellious youth in Mutare, invited me to. By day she was a primary-school teacher, but at night she huddled in smoky kitchens, helping to plot the demise of the 'forces of apartheid'. She would strip off her starched white blouse and long navy-blue skirt to don khaki trousers and a guerrilla-green camouflage beret. I envied her this ability to metamorphose, for I had no distinction now in my life between day and night. There was no duality, I was painfully singular in all I did. Her lifestyle frightened me and I cautioned her often of the perils of her underground activities, but she would laugh and cluck at me, 'Aluta continua, Sisi Shiri. The struggle is ours to fight; these boors are not going to hand us our independence.' I stayed clear of her friends. So you can imagine how reluctant I was to attend any parties with her. Many of them were fronts for political meetings anyway and several were raided by the Rhodesian police. This particular one was to celebrate the acquittal of our cousin Keki Thahane on charges of treason and terrorist activities against the Rhodesian government. Although I was ignorant of the details of his case, it was rumoured that he had been caught smuggling arms across the border to the freedom fighters in Mozambique. I had always liked Keki, although after he had moved out of Chakowa when we were teenagers, I had seen little of him. I had heard through Linda that he was now a high-ranking military commander in the armed struggle.

I met Linda at her flat in the nicer section of Sakubva. By the time we had picked up her gang of comrades and bought some beer, the party was in full swing. I recognized a few familiar faces but found myself often stranded alone near the snack bar. Keki came to my rescue.

'Shiri! What a surprise to see you.'

'I came to congratulate you, Keki.'

'Well, thanks.' He leaned against the table and looked into the dancing crowd. 'You know, Shiri, for a while I really doubted whether they would release me alive. And if they did, I was sure to spend the rest of my life in some caged cell, whipped and beaten daily by some *baas*.' I could find no adequate response. He drank his beer.

'Do you have a drink? Oh, that's right, I forgot, you're the good girl. Haven't you given up the sainthood yet?' He laughed and took another large swallow of his beer. He did not detect my wince. As if to confirm absolutely my priggishness, he pulled out a pack of cigarettes, mockingly offered me one and lit his. It was true that I had a reputation, despite my deviant relationship with the sculptor, of being the responsible and obedient one in our family. I drank no alcohol, fulfilled my filial duties without complaint, never smoked, and did not swear. I had even briefly flirted with the idea of joining the local Dominican sisters at their mission and becoming a missionary. I had once been naïve enough to believe that all would be well if you lived by the rules. Good things happened to good people, blessed are the meek, et cetera, et cetera. How disillusioned I have become since then. It hurt, because I wondered now what all that discipline, repression and suppression had been for if it had not procured me the thing I had most wanted, and it certainly did not guarantee happiness. Linda, on the other hand, had always been reckless. She had come home when she pleased; had constantly defied my parents; had had to be reminded to do her homework and her chores every single day. Even though there had only been three years' difference in our ages, I had literally brought her up as my own child. Yet she was the happy one. Linda had purpose. I saw her across the room, laughing up at her handsome dancing partner, stomping and thrusting her hips this way and that, in time to the thundering rhythm. Here I was, her elder sister, feeling awkward drinking a soft drink, being referred to as a good girl by a cousin her age. The sculptor remains my sole act of rebellious emotional independence. He was the only thing in my

127

youth that was truly mine. To love him was my choice; to give to him was my joy. All that I had done before and all I have done since feels oddly preplanned, like destiny unfolding. I have walked the path of blind faith except for that one brief digression. It is not that I do not love my life now and my home, for I do. It is just that for me, my sculptor was the road less travelled; he was the unknown, the possible, the mysterious and the beautiful. To my parents, however, he was an aberration in the otherwise straight path their dutiful daughter travelled.

'Linda has grown up so!' Keki exclaimed. 'She has great respect among the comrades. She's tough!' He was regarding her with a look of complete approval, which he reserved for very few people. I felt so far removed from this world. I felt as if I were living in a vacuum. At that moment, I was overcome by a feeling of such profound alienation that I longed to flee to the safety of my own familiar little flat at the Teachers' College. I got up from my chair to go.

'Shiri, you are not upset? I was only teasing about the sainthood thing.' Then suddenly shooting up and grabbing my elbow, he said, 'Oh look! Ha-ha! Here comes my partner – the man you should really congratulate for my release.' From among the dancers emerged a tall, very dark-skinned young man with a stout build and a tiny moustache. He moved with a confident grace that was rare among us in those days. We had been taught to be inferior for so long that even among ourselves we walked cautiously, with our heads down and our shoulders bent forward in resignation. I thought he looked vaguely familiar as he strode towards us, but I could not place him. The two men embraced warmly, slapping each other on the back, laughing all the while.

'How can I thank you, comrade, for the new life you

have given me?'

'Oh. Then clearly you have not yet received my bill,' laughed the one with the moustache. He then placed a firm grip on Keki's shoulder and in a deep, clear voice said, 'I trust that you will use your release to free the rest of us, my friend.' They fell to shaking hands and slapping each other on the back again. Then they raised their glasses.

'A toast,' said Keki, 'to certain victory!'

'*Aluta continua,*' added the moustached one solemnly before he drank.

It was only then that Keki seemed to remember my presence. I had actually been quite content to observe them. I knew I had not the energy to match theirs and I certainly was not in the mood for chitchat. I was about to slip quietly away. I was quite dismayed when Keki wheeled around and, apologetically taking my arm, presented me before his 'partner' and introduced us. That is how I met your father. My heart never skipped a beat. I did not stumble forward or stutter my words. I held my glass firmly and in one steady movement extended a hand of greeting. I was clear of vision and firm of foot. In fact, the longer we were together, the more stable my steps became, the clearer my vision, the steadier my hands, and the more lucid my thoughts. He became a constant in the complex equation of multiple variables that has characterized our lives.

Yet your father was never mine. He belonged to the domestic workers who marched through the wide city streets, on strike to demand better wages; the battered wife who knocked on the door, sobbing, at night; the displaced family that suddenly appeared on our doorstep at dawn; and the ubiquitous underground freedom fighters who frequented our house at night, speaking in low, determined whispers, and crept out by daybreak. Long before he had met me his passion and his heart had been wedded to the struggle. His commitment to his first love was absolute. Our courtship, for example, was entirely public. It could not have been otherwise. I would sit in some inconspicuous spot at seminars and briefings, listening to them plot and strategize; at rallies I distributed leaflets or sat beside him as he delivered thundering speeches that made my heart vibrate in my chest. In the evenings, we ate a hurried meal with his colleagues, fellow lawyers, freedom fighters and organizers. There were never any stolen moments. He was warm and compassionate in all that he did, but he understood that history was being made with every speech, every battle that we won, and every law that we defied and so rewrote. 'I stand before you not as a lawyer,' he would shout into the megaphone at his rallies, addressing hundreds of protesting students, journalists and peasants, 'but as a fellow writer and an editor. I am here to correct the errors of the system, to delete the injustices and to erase the lies that have been inserted and twisted in the living text of our own history. I am a soldier in the battle to defend and honour African truth. We are all editors, then, of our own history, and I invite you to join my army. I need no AK47 for this revolution, comrades, just a big mouth and a ballpoint!' At this, the crowd would roar in admiring laughter. He was a man of action, with no time for sentimentality. Curiously, this suited me perfectly. I was content to have such a friend and partner. It reminded me of the relationship between my mother and me in days gone by.

I admired in him the same tirelessness and selflessness that she had exhibited. Yet while her strength was invested in her handiwork, your father's power lay in his words. He could set them one after the other in such a heavy and damning manner that they became the lifelong prison term of a criminal; then when he chose, he arranged them in such a gentle and beguiling fashion that the bound were set free and the condemned were pardoned. I had watched him motivate masses of people, stir a crowd into frenzy and silence a courtroom at will, simply by selecting his tone, and by repeating one word here, thundering one there, and whispering another there – just so. To me, words were spoken and written. Lifeless things, they were necessary for everyday communication, but to your father, they are tangible tools: they are like the saw that brings down a towering ancient tree, the wrench that pries open a closed door, the brush that can paint a scene of wondrous beauty, the hammer that destroys the obsolete barrier or the key that unlocks the barbed cell. He had such a strength and confidence about him that I felt his balancing force wherever I was; like an anchor, he was that little extra weight that I needed to steady my course in the storms of life. And so he has remained to this day.

IX

Our first few years together were years of sleeplessness and hard work as the struggle became more organized. Those were strange days in Rhodesia. It was surreal. We all lived dual lives, except perhaps the Europeans. To the superficial white eye, all was tranquil. In the chic European suburbs, where we were forbidden to live, there were pristine lawns, scurrying maids and gardeners laughing behind the tall, shiny white gates of sprawling homes. Through the cracks in the fences one could discern the blue swimming pool catching the afternoon sun and the gleam of metal bouncing off the elegant cars that lined the driveway. It was a very insular world then for them. The Europeans stayed behind their concrete fences as if cement and steel were strong enough to bar the winds of change that howled and lashed at their hopeless fortresses of oppression. The newspapers warned everyone to be on the alert for terrorists who were trying to destabilize the country but they published not a word about the battles that raged daily in the bush. No ink was wasted on the tanks and troops that overran whole villages, killing our cattle, massacring our children. No one heard of the schoolgirls who were raped, the bush fires that the Rhodesian forces set alight, to smoke out the 'terrorist savages', and the homes of Africans that were razed to a few sticks of charcoal. The radio still blared soothing jazz from the Americas and glorious symphonies from Europe. All was well. All was under control. The taming of Africa was right on schedule.

At school the children were taught that Cecil Rhodes and his British South Africa Company discovered this land and the Europeans had wrought from the jungle the civilization that was Rhodesia. There were horrific posters at the petrol station, the shopping malls, and even at the church, caricaturing an African with thick lips and shifty eyes wielding an AK47 rifle in the face of a screaming (and presumably defenceless) white mother and babe. The caption read: 'Beware of terrorists. Arm your family.' Another read: 'Be prepared to fight.' The terrorists were depicted by the media as barbaric, bloodthirsty black anarchists. Thus European house-wives dutifully armed themselves. Pale, frightened schoolboys put away their khaki shorts and gilded blazers, fitfully joining the Rhodesian army to fight for what they believed was truly theirs.

Do you remember my cousin Tinawo Muti? She is now the head of the Office of National Intelligence in Mutare. She and Linda were about the same age and very close; even to this day they are virtually inseparable. Tinawo had the face of an angel, which was ironic because she was an unabashed liar – although not about important things. In fact she had not even been particu-larly naughty as a child. It was just that she could make up the grandest stories! She could thoroughly convince anyone of anything just with her sweet voice and those large, charcoal eyes. Even Reverend Chigare could never decide whether to believe her or not. Very early on her teachers stopped asking her why she was late or where she had been the day before because she weaved such an obtuse tale that one was at a complete loss as to how to interpret it. She was forever talking herself and Linda out of scrapes. She could play dumb as a stone but everyone knew she was frightfully clever. She disappeared from Chakowa just after our Form Two examinations. One day she was playing by the riverside with us and the next day she had completely vanished. Linda was inconsolable for months after she left. She spent hours in the afternoon sitting beneath the shade of the baobab tree by Sekuru Clever's plot, just staring into the mountains. In those days, many young boys and girls suddenly disappeared from the village. One speculated that either they had been captured by the Rhodesian army or they had crept over the border to Mozambique to join the struggle. They said nothing to their families. It was an act of charity to spare them the burden of knowledge which late one night in a raid they might have been beaten senseless to reveal.

I did not see Tinawo for almost four years. According to Linda she had been training at a camp outside Dar es Salaam in Tanzania. I was therefore quite surprised to see her at the shopping centre in Mount Pleasant one day. She was wearing the unmistakable starched pink uniform of a house girl and pulling a chubby, chattering white toddler by the hand. Perhaps the struggle had been too much. After all, one had family – brothers, sisters, parents and cousins – to look after. The village couldn't live by ideology and freedom songs alone, I supposed. I greeted her with genuine delight.

'Tinawo! How are you, stranger?' She appeared equally pleased and surprised to see me. We clasped hands warmly in greeting.

'Ay, Sisi Shiri. How are you? It is good to see you after so many years. How are the old folks?' she said, holding fast now to the child as he tried to wander off in the direction of the sweets.

'They are well, thanks. You must come home and see us sometime; we have just moved to Harare.'

'Oh! I forgot! Congratulations to you – you are married now! I admire your husband very much. He is doing much for our people.'

'Yes. He works too hard.' I scribbled our address on a piece of paper and handed it to her. 'And where are you these days, Tinana?'

She smiled to hear her childhood nickname. 'I am working for Commander Sir Charles Billingsworth Pelleday, chief of the Rhodesian air force.' She said it with great pride and a curious sardonic twist to her lips. 'This is his son, little Master Charles B. Pelleday the second.' The child refused to acknowledge me, despite Tinawo's coaxing. He tugged insistently on her hand. 'They live just around the corner. Linda comes frequently. You should come and see us there, Sisi.' She smiled with a wink. I watched her escort the little boy to purchase some lollipops and then they disappeared into a row of soaps, bleach and washing powder. How extraordinary, I remember thinking at the time, that one who had risked her life to get across the border (for there were land mines planted all over the frontier at the eastern highlands and it was jokingly said that when the Rhodesian troops saw a 'nigger' crossing the border, they shot first and asked questions at the post mortem) – she who had left her widowed mother and retarded brother to fend for themselves, who had forsaken all that was home, protected and familiar, for the rugged, thorny unknown of the African bush, all in the name of

135

freedom, and then spent two years studying and training in Tanzania at some army camp – could then just become a house girl. For that, she did not even need a primary-school education. I wondered, too, what she discussed with Linda, who was by now heavily politicized and working underground full-time.

Those were the days when Linda grew thin, like a stick. She ate, breathed and lived for the struggle. It was her life. I saw her sometimes when she came in the company of other comrades in fatigues and dark glasses to consult with your father, drop off pamphlets or use the telephone. Sometimes she would just come to 'crash'. We tried to feed her, protect her as best we could on those occasions, but as soon as her strength returned she donned her beret and fled back to a world that I only saw in fragments and whispers. It is funny, but I sometimes think it was Linda who was meant to marry your father – they are made from the same substance; their spirits are the same parts of some greater whole. I understood this and so never questioned them when they closed the study door and stayed for hours whispering in hushed tones, mapping out strategies, writing communiqués and speeches. Their commitment to the struggle was absolute and their integrity beyond reproach.

The next time I saw Tinawo was eight months later, back in Chakowa, where the entire clan was gathered for Mbuya Amai Byron's eightieth birthday. This coincided with Easter so the whole village was in a festive mood: there were plays at the chapel, parties and feasts planned at every house, and the shops offered a full stock of fizzy, coloured soft drinks, sticky sweets and jam-filled buns. The shop windows glowed welcomingly in the evening, adorned with rows of bright Christmas lights which blinked asynchronously. We were determined to make it a memorable celebration for the old woman. I think we all, in our own way, tried to make up to her for the absence of her son, Mukoma Byron. Linda, Tinawo and I were assigned the task of preparing the goat meat and the vegetables. I chose a spot at the back of the yard with a view of the valley, right under the leafy cover of an avocado tree, for the three of us to sit. I laid the *machira* down for a mat and set the large enamel dishes at the centre. Tinawo and Linda came bounding out of the hut, carrying the cut-up beast in an enormous metal pot, waving away flies as they approached. As always, their conversation was loud and animated, punctuated by eruptions of uninhibited guttural laughter that brought tears to their eyes and made them hold their bellies in agony.

'What are you talking about, you two? Mind not to spill the meat! Besides, if it is that funny, then you must share it,' I said as they set the pot down unsteadily and we set to work.

'Sisi, we were just talking about the Europeans. You know, they are really wonderful! They honestly believe that we come from monkeys and they come from God.' I was surprised to hear Linda say this so cheerfully.

'And so they think we are stupid,' added Tinawo.

'What is so wonderful about that?' I asked them as I separated strips of tripe from the rest of the meat.

'You see, Sisi, our greatest weapon in the struggle has been our presumed stupidity. The Europeans do not believe that we have brains of any evolutionary significance. So, as far as they are concerned, our capacity for rational thought is, shall we say, ahh, limited!' Tinawo explained, fighting back giggles. 'They do not believe, based upon all their collected scientific data, that a native African could ever think rationally, or develop any sort of military or political strategy, and so they do not really take us seriously.'

'Thank God,' added Linda. 'After all the blunders you have made, Tinana, I bet they still do not suspect you! Remember the time when your Commander Bigot caught the three of us, Mukoma Keki, George and I, fully dressed in army fatigues in your room? Hey! Tinana can tell stories! Sisi Shiri, you should have heard her tell her master how these terrorists had wandered into her compound to try to indoctrinate her and how she had told them to leave and they refused. He would have killed her had he guessed the truth. The situation was so obviously fishy, and, no offence, Tinana, but your entire explanation was preposterous. Sisi Shiri, you should have seen the way she clung to her *baas*, Commander Pelleday, her big black eyes wide with fright, and begged him to make us go away. Hey! And the way we got chased off that property, I tell you! Ayee! That *baas* of yours, Tinana, almost shot George in the leg. He barely missed, and I almost got bitten by those hounds of his. And all the time, as we were running for our lives, we could hear the clear voice of Tinawo shouting, "Get out of here, you bloody terrorists!" If only he could have known that it was his poor innocent little maid who was the one passing on information to *us* and planning the next day's strategy in Mazoe Province. Ah! but you, Tinana, you are too much.' They were clutching their sides in laughter, remembering the scene. I shook my head, finally putting it all together. So Tinawo had not abandoned the struggle.

'Oh, Tinawo, so you are still fighting. I didn't know what to think when I saw you at the shops.'

'Still fighting?' flashed Linda indignantly. 'She is a commander, Sisi Shiri. That is why we matched her with

Pelleday, or "Commander Bigotsworth" as she calls him. When she is feeling particularly affectionate, she calls him simply Bigot. How do you think we find out about the secret plans of the Rhodesian forces? Little do they know that Commander House Girl is relaying everything to the bush.' She chuckled, pleased with her play of words, as she cut the meat into little strips and threw them into a second pot full of onions, tomatoes and seasonings. And so we spent the morning recounting stories of war and childhood. I admit some of Tinawo's stories were terrifying. But there she was, with a face as sweet as a baby's, living every day in the precarious employ of her enemy, as a spy. Unbelievable. I marvelled at them. So these were the women of the struggle. These were the women who by their bravery and sacrifice would become the heroes of the future.

'But, Tinana, are you not frightened?' I asked.

'Sisi, the only time I was really terrified, and that day I was shaking, was several months ago. The commander always leaves his top-secret papers and the tapes he has from the tapped phones of our guys, in the safe by his desk in the study. Initially, they absolutely forbade me to enter that room. It was not until after the first month when I acted so stupid in all that I did that they let me in to dust and polish. It was great those first few days. Whenever the madam wrote out any instructions for me, I always did the opposite. So, finally, she figured that I could not read. When they asked me about the war, I told them that I didn't understand why there was fighting when we had all lived so peacefully and happily for so long together. They were so pleased with that "precious native philosophy" that Mrs Pelleday patted my hand and said with glowing approval, "You are a very sensible girl. Don't you listen to what those other foolish

Africans say."

' "No, madam," I said, and stole away quickly before I burst into laughter. Anyway, every day I would dust his office. I always timed it with madam's visit to the hair and beauty parlour, the gardening or bridge game, so that I could take my time. Then I would lock the door, close the curtains, and carefully go through all the files on his desk. I would photograph and copy as much as I could. Commander Bigot never came home during the day. He prided himself on being a man of steel discipline. He could often be heard expounding to Victory, for so the unfortunate gardener is named, "All you need is discipline, my dear boy. Your people would make the finest workers if only you could be more disciplined, more controlled. Why, it is the very mark of civilization, don't you know. The evolved man can tame his basic instincts; the barbarian is ruled by them." Victory understood perfectly what he meant, for he himself was ruled by the bottle. Victory was an absolute drunkard. From the moment that he collected his pay on Friday at 3 p.m. and leapt over the fence and across the fields to the nearest bar until late Monday morning when he returned to work, he was blissfully stuporous. Yet they never fired him. Instead, he was sternly lectured to by Madam Bigot every Monday morning as he staggered among the rose bushes, clipping unsteadily, then invariably sent to the compound to sober up with a large plastic container of thick black coffee. Their sermons were entirely wasted on the poor fellow, whose English vocabulary comprised about twelve words including *trim, cut, prune, beer, cigarettes, madam, master* and *yes, please*. He had never bothered to learn to say thank you, so whenever he was given anything or offered some kindness he said with a winning grin, "Yes, please!" They said that he was extremely good-natured and never took offence. Well, it was no wonder! He understood not one word they said. He amused us all and diverted much attention away from my more devious tasks.

'Mondays were perfect because madam focused all her attention on Victory in the morning and then went out in the afternoon. I knew the commander would not return until 6.40 p.m. exactly. The cook, whom we affectionately dubbed Sekuru Chef, jokingly said that you could set your clock by the commander's schedule. In any case madam never went near his study so I felt quite safe. As soon as I heard madam slam the garden door and walk towards the rose bushes with a familiar shrill "Now, Victory, if I have told you once, I have told you a thousand times . . . ," that was my cue. I would stealthily enter the commander's study and lock the door behind me. For weeks I had been trying to crack the code of his safe. I finally felt that I had the right combination. He often opened it in my presence while I pretended to be absorbed in dusting his desk or polishing the furniture. I snapped shots of the various memos on his desk and then crawled underneath it to reach the safe box. I was ecstatic when after several turns I heard a little click and the door creaked open. Inside were the papers I had heard of from Brigadier Hamani at our meeting in Mazoe but had not been able to locate anywhere among Bigot's files. I leafed through them and began to lay them out on the floor to snap them. I closed the safe door to give myself room and set to work photographing. I must have been too absorbed to hear the jeep drive in. I only remember feeling a chill to my toes when just outside the study window I heard the deep, sharp voice of my employer shouting at the dog which was barking ferociously.

'"Down, boy! Down! Is this any way to greet a

lieutenant of the army?" I then discerned the laughter of another, younger male voice. Next I heard the slamming of doors and footsteps headed in my direction. I felt at that moment as if my entire body was overtaken by my heart, whose pulses sent searing, paralysing electric jolts through each and every nerve in my body. I had no time to open the safe and stuff the papers inside and I was trapped under the desk. I folded and crumpled the papers into two pads and stuffed them down my brassière. Luckily for me, those uniforms are made for the thick, busty *ambuyas* so there was plenty of room. Just as I adjusted my uniform and tried to formulate a plan, I heard the key turn in the door and I caught sight of two pairs of black boots as they stepped into the room – one enormous shiny pair followed by a smaller, more worn set. One pair stepped to the far wall, away from me.

‘ "Want a drink, lieutenant?" I recognized the unmistakable authoritarian bark of my employer and associated him with the giant feet. He opened a handsome cabinet and poured two glasses of whiskey.

‘ "No, sir. I never drink during the day."

‘ "Very wise, son. Very wise. I am glad to know that these papers will be passed on to such a level-headed fellow. I know that they will reach Commander David and the troops on the front lines. You understand, then, how important these documents are, son. They have top-secret information for coordinating our strategy. This is the master plan, a copy, naturally, of the original at headquarters.'

‘ "Yes, sir, I do," said Small Boots, shifting nervously from one foot to the other.

‘ "Well then, son, how about a smoke?"

‘ "Thank you, sir. I'll have a cigarette." I heard the shaking of a matchbox, a strike and the soft crackling of a lit cigarette.

'"Sit down, son. At your ease. Let me get you a soft drink. If I can find our maid, that is." Big Boots strode to the door and gruffly called my name as he disappeared out into the corridor. I could hear the drumming of his heavy feet as he headed towards the kitchen. I must have made a move, unwittingly. Small Boots leapt up, and in a split second I heard the deafening crackle of shotgun fire and I leaped forward as the bullet whizzed past my head and shattered the door of the safe. I hit the centre coffee table and found my face in the ashtray, a glowing cigarette and a box of matches at my elbow. I could hear the commander's boots racing back, and an incredulous, "What in the name of God . . .?"

'I was in a desperate situation. This would be a tough one to talk myself out of. If they found me out, I knew I would hang, Sisi. I could almost hear the papers in my breast rustle with each deafening pound of my heart and the pressure of the little camera in my apron pocket burned into my thigh. I saw my only escape in a split second before the commander reached the doorway and while the stunned, short, blond lieutenant stared at his gun in disbelief. In a flash, I seized some of the unimportant papers that had fallen in the flurry, threw them into the safe and threw a match into it. At precisely that second, the commander reached the door and the young officer looked up – first at me, then at his superior officer.

'"What in the name of God?" he repeated, this time much more slowly. Then, as the smoke rose from the safe he took full control.

'"The papers, God damn it. Save the papers!" The young man reached for the water jug from the bar and threw it into the safe. I ran off, pretending to fetch more water, but I leaped over the fence to my quarters and buried the papers and the camera in a metal safe of my own that I kept beneath the toilet. I returned, breathless, with a bucket of soap and water and splashed it all over the commander's carpet and the safe. I reached into the safe, scratching my forearms, and made sure that not a shred of identifiable paper remained. What few leaves remained I clumped together in a tight fist and wrung dry only to dump the amorphous clod back into the water. They would never be able to tell that the soggy mass was not actually the top-secret papers that Small Boots had come for. I wanted to flee again, but the young man gripped my shoulder and pushed me roughly back onto the floor.

'"You woolly-headed little kafir, what the hell were you doing there?" he spat into my face. His face was like a ripe tomato at harvest except that rather than a smooth shiny skin, his was blotchy and twisted in hate.

'"What exactly happened, lieutenant?" asked the commander in a voice that crackled with thunder. His face was stony, but his eyes were ablaze with fury.

'"Sir, I heard a sound beneath the table there, and when I saw her face, I thought it was a spy . . . or one of the terrorists." His eyes turned sharply towards me and gleamed such an icy blue that I felt the blood in my body freeze. I, of course, turned my face down and began to snivel and sob helplessly. Small Boots delivered a very powerful kick to my right flank, and he growled, "Shut up! Get up, you sneaky kafir!" He hoisted me up and shook me furiously before Bigot. "What the hell were you doing in here, eh?" he persisted.

'Several of the other servants had come running and had now gathered silently at the door of the study, their curiosity curbed by the ominous scene before them. The gun must have caused quite a blast, for after a few minutes even Victory came staggering to the door swaying slightly from side to side and rubbing his bloodshot eyes. It was one of his loud hiccups that drew attention to the group. The commander turned to them and said in a voice of thin control, "Back to your duties, all of you." They disbanded, casting me mournful glances, for my predicament seemed to assure a grisly – although, thankfully, immediate – death. Small Boots was still brandishing his weapon menacingly in my direction. We all knew that one African life was insignificant to the Europeans. It was one less beggar in the street, one less grass hut dotting the countryside, and one less bothersome terrorist to fight. Some even considered it a public service to rid the world of our backward existence in times of war – or peace, for that matter. The African hunting season flourished all year long in those days. The issue of guilt was of course irrelevant and a trial was out of the question. Honestly, Sisi Shiri, I kept thinking that I really didn't mind dying for the struggle; I just didn't want to end my life in such an insignificant way. After all this, it seemed pathetic to be caught out in Mount Pleasant, one of the poshest white suburbs in Harare, on a sunny afternoon in an oak-panelled study at the hands of some low-level Rhodesian youth. Death was something we always knew could come in the struggle. But I had always prayed to die in the bush, close to the earth, with my red blood sinking into and forever staining the land that I was fighting for. And if I could not meet my Maker on my own soil, then I wished to gasp my last breath facing Kilimanjaro or wading through the undergrowth of the Mozambiquan forest. This was a dishonourable death. Imagine dying ensconced in colonialist treasures, on a fluffy pink carpet beneath an eighteenth-century French desk. It was too much.

'"Search her,' said the commander indifferently.

'To my great distress Small Boots began to thrust his hands gruffly under my uniform, over my back, under my blouse, over my buttocks (a little too slowly, I might add) and over my belly, leaving several black-and-blue weals. Look, Linda, you can still see this scar on my arm. He was visibly disappointed to find nothing at all except an old shopping list. The commander was now looking out at the garden and smoking a cigarette.

'"Is that how they train you out there?"

'"Sir?"

'"I said, is that how they train you out there in Gwelo?"

'"Yes, sir. We are told to shoot first and ask questions later, sir. The Africans are full of tricks and magic, sir. We never let them get close to us."

'There was no response from his superior.

'"Shall I take her to headquarters, sir?"

'"To do what?"

'"Sir?"

'"Look at her, man!" Small Boots once again turned in my direction.

'"The girl has been in my employ for over a year. I checked her references thoroughly. In the entire twelve months, she has not displayed one whit of intelligence. She cannot read. And God knows, she can barely write out the grocery list. She has to be guided through the simplest instructions. I do not think my wife could have found a more perfect house girl had she combed the country for the thickest native she could find."

'"But sir . . ."

'"Come on, lieutenant. Surely you don't think she is a

spy. Did she have any weapon? Were there any incriminating materials on her? And for whom would she be spying? For what? Trust me, her political interests are confined to whether or not she can afford to buy mealie meal to make *sadza*."

'The lieutenant released his grasp of me and I collapsed in a little whimpering heap at the centre of the study.

' "Get up, girl. Go and clean yourself up and get back to work."

' "Yes, sir," I said. I was careful not to leap out of the room, but to drag myself in a sorry fashion to the door. I picked up the bucket of soap and water and managed clumsily to spill it on the little boots, then say softly, "Oh, dear. Oh, dear. I am sorry about your shoes, sir. Oh my! Madam will be cross with me for getting the carpet wet."

'The lieutenant stared at me in disbelief. I think he was trying to decide whether to strangle me then and there for being a devious little spy or feel pity for my utter, impenetrable stupidity as a house girl. Thank God Bigot had already drawn his own conclusions.

' "You see, my man; she has not the slightest inkling of what is happening. Daft as a wooden plank. The very epitome of her profession – I daresay her race!" The commander chuckled.

'Small Boots was not so amused. He raised his gun to my head as I reached the door, and said, "If you are ever caught snooping in the commander's papers again, there will be a bullet through your head."

'I overcame the fear, inspired by the cool metal against my temple, and responded sweetly, "I was only dusting, sir. Madam said to make sure the room shines. She gets quite cross with me if I don't follow orders, sir."

'At this the commander smiled, and it seemed even the

lieutenant began to believe, finally, that I was indeed an imbecile.

' "Get out of my sight!"

' "Yes, sir!" I said to the tomato blond with the shiny little boots. Then, addressing the commander, I said, "Shall I bring you some tea, sir, or a drink?"

' "No. Just leave us in peace, my girl," he said impatiently. Then he added sarcastically, "Go and make the other rooms shine."

' "Yes, sir," I exclaimed with alacrity, and closed the door behind me. I heard a loud burst of laughter from both men as I left. But I know that the tomato-blond lieutenant received a stern warning from Bigot and a lecture on discipline and the dangers of starting a fire from shooting recklessly indoors because Sekuru Chef brought them sandwiches later and repeated every word that he overheard. The other servants were incredulous to see me going about my business as usual that afternoon. They thought for certain that I would emerge in cuffs and chains and be carted off, never to be heard of again. They plagued me with questions for months afterwards. All I ever told them was that I had been dusting under the table, got scared when they entered the room, thinking they were burglars, and that as soon as the commander left, the younger man had taken fright and shot at me as I tried to crawl out and reveal myself. That was all. I trusted no one in times of war, for one never knew the true allegiances of another's heart. Some wanted freedom, but only if others fought for it for them. Then there were the misguided few who had sold their souls for a few sacks of mealie meal and meat and become the informers to the Rhodesian forces. I pretended to go about my business as a dim house girl. Many of my fellow slaves in Bigot's household did not realize what we had to gain from independence and some actually believed the white lies. The simpler ones also believe that I am irreparably brain-damaged; a few, like Sekuru Chef, suspect that it is a front, but they do not interfere.

'I was still permitted to enter the study. Ironically, in fact, if anything they were more lax in their supervision, as they believed that I was genuinely, impenetrably dense and therefore thoroughly trustworthy. The papers eventually reached Commander Bigot's troops but the freedom fighters received them a good five days before the Rhodesian forces and so foiled yet another Joint Forces Mission.'

I saw the smile that spread across Linda and Tinawo's faces as they recalled their victories. Tinawo had now warmed to her subject and I shifted on the cloth to make myself comfortable. We were sure to get a few more good stories before our task was done. We did not have to wait long, for soon Tinawo let out a chuckle.

'Oh! I cannot forget the day that I understood at last that the Europeans in our country would never understand the heart of the African. And I understood why so many thousands before me had given up trying to make the whites understand with entreaties, talks and demands and had finally, sometimes reluctantly, taken to the bush with missiles, rifles and bombs. I was serving tea to them by the pool, on a beautiful day in November last year, almost as hot as today. Seated beside Commander Pelleday was a tall, thin Englishman, representing one of the papers overseas, who had come to interview him. I milled around as best I could to catch pieces of the interview. As I approached with the tray, I could hear that the commander was getting angry – he rarely raised his voice at home – so I was especially curious. I kept pretending to forget things like the sugar, the spoons, the milk and so on. Happily, I had acted so foolishly throughout my employ that I raised no suspicions whatsoever. As I was stirring the cream in his tea, Bigot turned to me and, seizing my hand, swung me to the thin man's side.

'"Here. Now here is a typical African. Look, man, can you imagine her governing this country? Would you trust her to run your economic policy? Your military? Can you imagine this uneducated girl as an army commander? Well? You people over there simply do not understand our Africans. They are not the sophisticated lot you have over there, all those big athletes and superstars. These are bush people!" All this time his grip never loosened; in fact, he was shaking me to and fro as if I were a puppet, almost as if to show the man that I was not even real.

'"But surely there are others, the ones leading the struggle, the freedom fighters—" the reporter began.

'"Freedom fighters!" spat the commander. "My God, man, those are Communists! Nothing but savage terrorists with Soviet machinery set to wreak anarchy, I tell you. I have seen them on the frontiers. They don't care a damn about freedom. Look at her – she's free. That's Rhodesia." He shook me more vigorously still.

'"But what do you think of Africans voting?"

'"Well, now, for years, they have had the right to vote amongst themselves in their villages, among the tribes, about matters that concern their chiefs. But surely you're not suggesting that they be allowed to vote at a national level? We have to get them up to our level first. We have to teach them our long history of democracy." At this point, he let me go with such a shake that I was flung aside. As I teetered to regain balance, the tray that I had been holding scattered dotting their perfect lawn with chocolate éclairs, coconut creams and cinnamon orange squares. Commander Bigotsworth continued without a blink as I scrambled to pick up the cakes and biscuits.

'"I am not saying it's impossible, but it will take years and years. They are ignorant! Look here." He beckoned me back as I slowly fetched one biscuit after the other while unsuccessfully fighting off the dog. He raised a telegram that I had handed him earlier that day announcing the arrival of the reporter. I stared at it blankly. "Now, what does this say?" he asked smugly, not even looking at me at all, but keeping his eyes on the newspaperman's expression.

'"I do not know, sir."

'"You see, Mr Thorn. Now how can someone like this be expected to vote? Ideology would only confuse her. These people are uneducated. They are not ready yet. No, not for years yet. We know *our* Africans. They are very simple, very innocent people. They like to eat their little bit of *sadza* and meat, drink a little beer now and again, sleep under a shady tree in the noonday sun, and produce lots of children. Nothing more."

'The young man tried to interrupt but the commander continued.

'"But we are open to change. We are not the unreasonable people the English believe. We do foresee a day when we have two culturally appropriate systems to govern our country – one for the Africans and one for us. Each according to his capacity. Isn't that what the Bible says, Mr Thorn?"

'The poor young man was extremely uncomfortable and kept glancing at me apologetically, as if somehow the entire situation, from Rhodes's arrival to Ian Smith's governance, had been his doing.

'"Well, sir, it just seems to me that the Africans, being

the truly indigenous peoples and outnumbering the Europeans by millions, should have the right to govern themselves."

'"No!" thundered Bigotsworth. He slammed his fist down so hard that all the cups shook from their saucers and I had to dash to save the cream and sugar from spilling. "Not in my lifetime. There will never be majority rule in Rhodesia! Do you hear me loud and clear, young man? Not while we still have guns and tanks to fight. Not while young men are willing to join in defence of their land. We have families, farms and businesses to protect. We are here to stay, Mr Thorn. You tell the world out there that never, ever will the European live under the governance of savages. It goes against the rules of evolution. It is preposterous."

'This last outburst set the poor fellow scribbling frantically on his thick yellow pad. "But how long will the war go on for?" he gasped, his face flushed with excitement, looking up swiftly as he turned a page of his pad.

'"War? There is no war. We are simply in a prolonged state of emergency that requires us to be vigilant. What you are referring to are bush skirmishes. Those boys are not disciplined fighters – they have no training. They have no plan, man. I tell you, old chap, we shall have them all exterminated in six months. What they need is a fine hiding and then to be put to some useful work." He laughed confidently. "Pity is, I won't have the job then. I shall have to go down to South Africa and lend a hand. The Zulu there are getting restless too, I hear. You know what they say, 'Rhodesians never die, they just move south.' Heh, heh."

'"But it is said that the freedom – er, the African fighters are gaining footage in the eastern highlands near the border with Mozambique."

'"Nonsense! Sheer bravado propaganda by the terrorists! They have absolutely no support from the peasants, who, as I told you already, are content in their tribal trust lands. There they have a little plot where they can grow their vegetables and raise as many children as they like. They have no ear for the terrorists' slogan of 'One Man, One Vote'. Go out and see them. The Africans are always laughing. They were very happy with the way things were before those bloody Communists started to stir up trouble."

'"But sir, how do they survive if the people in the rural areas do not feed, clothe and hide them?" asked the reporter bravely. My *baas* gave him a sharp look of disbelief.

'"Surely you are aware of their methods. They beat their own poor people and steal wantonly. These are no soldiers, my boy. These are petty criminals without promise or purpose. But we will stop them and restore peace to Rhodesia."

'I was now being pursued steadily by the dog, who sniffed and nibbled at my ankles, and you know how dogs frighten me. I edged towards the commander's seat, and as the dog barked furiously, I trembled so, the china clinked on the tray. On seeing my terror, the commander beckoned his dog and barked at it, "Sit!" The miserable beast obeyed and he stroked it affectionately. There was nothing more satisfying and reassuring to him than absolute obedience. He looked afresh at Mr Thorn with a triumphant smile, as if some major issue had been settled, some global truth revealed.

'"You see? These people are like children. They need to be guided and taken care of. These Africans have among the best standards of living in the world. That is because we look after them. For years they have been contented. And now a few misguided thugs are determined to destroy everything we have worked so hard to build. Look around. As you travel through the cities and the bush you will see the extraordinary beauty of Rhodesia. It is a land worth fighting for."

'At this, his wife, who had sat in silence throughout, reached out and stroked his hand affectionately. "You see, Mr Thorn, my husband was born here and his father built this house." She pointed to the gardens, the gleaming windows of the balcony of their bedroom, which overlooked the lawn, the bamboo trees, the stables that peeked from the woods in the distance and the pool whose gentle current made a soothing sound. "Rhodesia is all he knows. They say that Africa belongs to the blacks, but that's not true. It's not fair. We have made this our home. We belong here too. We'll be damned if we are going to just hand over everything we have. Our whole lives have been spent in fashioning a life out of this jungle. If they want a country, let them build one. We are not giving up ours. Can you people not understand that? So many of the English papers nowadays support the Africans and they don't ever see our point of view. It is really not fair."

'Mr Thorn was able to avoid answering her by plunging his wiry neck into his pad and resuming writing at a furious pace. The Rhodesians shook their heads sadly, feeling as if they could not make themselves understood. He eventually looked up, wiped the crumbs of tea cake from his lap and, folding his pad into his little leather satchel, thanked them for their time.

'"You will send us a copy of the article, won't you?" asked Mrs Pelleday as he was leaving. Mr Thorn hesitated.

'"Er, why, of course. Of course. I am sure you will find my article, er, very er, interesting." With an ironic smile and a wave he drove off.

'As I was clearing the table outside I overheard them mumble something about "meddling foreigners" and I heard the commander say gruffly, "They are such hypocrites. They think they can come down here and tell us what to do with our blacks, yet over there they treat their kafirs no better!"

'I felt so many things that night. As I went about my evening chores of washing the dishes, bathing young Master Pelleday and putting him to bed, I had to hide the bitterness. I knew then without any doubt that the armed struggle was our only road to freedom. I felt it in my heart that we must fight, by any means necessary, to regain the land of our ancestors.'

'These whites!' chimed in Linda, her face twitching with disgust. 'King Lobengula let them take some gold, but that was not enough. Now they are growing roots like a tree and claiming the very soil as their own.'

'Wait, Linda, I have not finished the story. Just before I locked up and went to my compound the commander called me to the sitting room, where they were having a "nightcap".

'As always, I knelt down in their presence, as was the custom whenever master or madam beckoned. He began with his back to me, staring out through the window at the garden. "Listen, my girl. We want to tell you about what is going on in this country, for your own good, so that you are not led astray. It will be very confusing for you with so many lies being told," he said in a heavy voice, puffing his cigar at the night air.

'Mrs Pelleday was seated at the far corner of their sitting room, by the bar. She sipped her drink and added,

"There are many bad people out there who are called terrorists because they frighten people, they beat them and kill people – African people – for no reason. They want to take away our land and our jobs and make Rhodesia poor like the other African countries." I wondered who was included in this ubiquitous "our".

'"We are trying to stop them. That is why the Rhodesian troops are fighting every day. You must be very careful. Trust no one and keep everything you hear in this house to yourself or you will find yourself in very bad trouble. If you need anything, ask us. We will take care of you as we always have. Do not be afraid, my girl. Soon everything will be calm and happy again like it used to be before this nasty business started."'

'Oh! That is good!' Linda burst in, unable to keep from interrupting. It was too much for her. 'Tinana, you should have said in that sweet voice of yours—' Linda got on her knees, mockingly clasped her hands together as if in prayer and crawled close to Tinawo, '"Oh, yes, sir, there is just one little, tiny thing I would like very much now that you mention it. How about freedom from your oppression? How about the right to vote or live where I please? How about the right to determine my life and that of my family? Perhaps the right to an education? Oh, yes, please sir, thank you for asking, how about a decent wage? Or even a toilet instead of the hole in the ground that you built for me as part of the little hovel you generously call my 'quarters'."'

Tinawo waved Linda away with an onion. 'Linda, what makes me sad is that I truly believe that the old lady and the old man meant what they said. They really felt that it was their duty to protect me. They really believed that I was happy to sleep in that stinking hovel that they provided as my compound. It never really occurred to them that my back might ache from lying on the hard, cold, cement floor covered by one of their old blankets with moth holes and cigarette burns and patches of old yellow stains as a bed. In their minds I was content to bathe cramped in a corner, crouched in a bucket, shivering as the cold water splashed over my body on frosty June mornings. They saw me as a domesticated animal no better than their dog. The conditions that they provided were perfectly appropriate for my level of civilization, or lack thereof. The dog at least got to sleep in the house, sit by the fire, and watch television, all privileges that were strictly forbidden to us Africans, and would be seen as signs of the servants being too free.'

'Tinana, how can you compare yourself to the white man's dog? Don't you know the animal is precious to his owner? A dog is, after all, a respectable member of the family – man's best friend, haven't you heard? Or, more accurately – white man's best friend. You, on the other hand, are nothing to him, an ignorant house girl, a barefoot, giggling domestic, a kafir, a nigger, a lowly jungle bunny.' Linda scorned, spewing back the hatred that she had heard hurled at her all these years. It took Linda some time, even after Independence, to rid herself of the gnawing bitterness of the constitutionalized racism that had so broadly defined and limited our education, our laughter, our play – in fact, our very lives as African children had been circumscribed by our colour. We were relegated to tribal trust lands; we attended Grade B or African schools; we could only shop at certain places, see certain sights, taste certain pleasures.

Can you imagine a system so thorough that even pain and enjoyment were strictly segregated along racial lines? If you were African, you had indigenous pleasures and you knew native pain. If you were Rhodesian, you experienced white pleasures and had your own particular set of European pain. That is apartheid at its best. You live in one space yet you inhabit different worlds. In that ingenious construct there can be no dialogue. None of us ever rebelled against the intellectually and spiritually debilitating confinement of Rhodesia so vigorously as my little sister Linda. She fought that system with her whole heart, her mind, and every fibre of physical strength that her body could recruit. Linda hated everything that colonialism and apartheid represented. But she saved her greatest loathing for its perpetrators. She had absolutely no tolerance for the misguided paternalism of the Europeans – zero. After suffering much, she won in the end. She is sitting, triumphant, in Mutare today, presiding over a multiracial staff. She tore down the walls that kept her in. But that day, we had no such immediate victory in sight. Linda was full of venom for the like of the Pelledays. I watched her seethe as she worked.

'Oh, you have reminded me of a good one!' Tinawo shook her head, smiling, pulling her bright green and red *jira* over her toes and fastening it more snugly around her hips. She took up the knife and began gingerly peeling a stack of potatoes. Still smiling, she began. 'I shall never forget the first day that I started working for the Pelledays. The old lady asked me to accompany her to the shops to fetch some vegetables and so she could introduce me to the grocer, butcher and baker. That way, she explained, she could send me to charge things to their account in the future without a hassle. As we walked up to the truck, which she told me she favoured for such errands, she opened the passenger door and, thinking her kind, I slipped in and installed myself in the front seat. She stood there with the door ajar and said to me awkwardly, "Oh, Charlie usually likes the front seat. He doesn't get out much, you know. He loves to have the wind in his hair and look out the window. Why don't you climb into the back?"

'I was naturally embarrassed, thinking that I should have realized that one of their children would be coming along, although I had not heard of one named Charlie. But you know how funny their names are, they call Robert Bob and William Bill. So, I tried to make myself comfortable on the rough ridges of the cool metal floor of the pick-up, clinging to the sides for security, and waited curiously to meet Charlie. I have seen the offences heaped upon us by the colonialists, but nothing in all my years at the mercy of jeering white hate prepared me for the sight of Charlie as he came bounding and barking around the hedge and flopped into the front seat to the affectionate giggles and kisses of Mrs Pelleday.

'"Oh, you naughty thing. Yes bi-i-ig doggy, you are so-o-o excited for the ride, aren't you?" she cooed, frisking his hair and burying her face in his abundant white fur.

'And so it was that at every outing we took, Charlie and Mrs Bigot sat in the front and I got to be frozen, tossed and bumped about in the open rear of their pick-up truck. It was an insult that I have never, ever, to this day, got over. Each time I hitch myself up and climb into the back and watch that shaggy mutt hop onto the cushioned front seat like a prince, I wonder what these Europeans really think of us. Perhaps it is good, because the experience never let me grow soft. Each Friday when we set off for the market, while the wind bubbles through my clothes and tickles my bones, while my knuckles turn maroon and blistered from clinging to the side railings as we swerve here and there, each time she opens the door for Charlie and leaves me to clamber and jump from the back without assistance, scraping my knees as I graze the edges of the railings, scampering to catch up with them while they trot off ahead, each time she meets a friend and introduces Charlie and leaves me as unmentionable as a ghost, I chant to myself, *Aluta continua*. This is why there is an armed struggle. For no kindness those people showed me was ever close to erasing the blow of that constant reminder that to them, for all their professed paternal benevolence, in their heart and at their hearth, they prefered a smelly, dirty dog rather than an African for company. How can one human being put an animal above his fellow man?'

Tinawo grew silent for several minutes. The story was touching but not unique. In those days it was common to see a white man and his dog riding in the front seat while his staff of Africans huddled in the open wagon of a truck. It was the natural order of things in Rhodesia.

I was tying the tripe very carefully one by one and laying them side by side in the big dish at the centre that was full of seasonings. Nearby a group of children were raising a film of red dust as they darted from one shrub to the next, squealing as they fell upon one another in a heap, only to leap up and chase each other to the next tree. Over the hedge I could see Granny Patience hanging her stringy sheets to dry. She waved to us and we all waved back. Down in the valley the little girls appeared like ants, balancing urns of water on their heads and carrying a bucket in each hand as they zig-zagged through the thorny bush that led to the main path. I could hear them giggling and singing their Sunday-school songs.

When Tinawo spoke again, she too was looking at the line of young girls, now jostling each other and challenging each other's balance on the path below us. In a distant voice, she said, 'Do you know why I joined the struggle, Sisi Shiri?'

I shook my head and continued very slowly to twist the tripe into neat squares and ribbons.

'I joined the freedom fighters because I wanted a dress. That is all. At fifteen, I simply wanted a pink dress with white flowers.'

I stopped what I was doing and turned to look her square in the face, expecting to meet there one of her foolish grins, but instead I saw her head was turned away from me, looking towards the girls. Her voice had lost its mirth.

'My father had promised me that if I did well in my exams he would buy me whatever I wanted. But he died in an ambush the year before I entered Form Two. He believed so strongly that education was the key to our freedom. As he passed me, sitting finishing my homework at the kitchen table in the evenings, he would say, "Let the candles burn late and long, my daughter, until you have eaten full of the white man's knowledge. Then and only then will this land be ours again."

'His job at the post office paid very little but he spent his last cents on my uniforms, my books, my paper and my bus fare. He used to tease me and ask me what did I want more than anything. And what I wanted was the dress that I had seen at the European store on Fourth Street – you know, the one in Mutare, next to the record shop. It sells pretty, clean, shiny things, not all stacked together in a dusty heap like at the Indian store. It had paintings and gold from South Africa, machira from Tanzania and fine, carved wooden boxes from Mozambique. I used to go past the window on Saturdays to gaze at this dress. I worked so hard for it. I stayed up late reading that chemistry book with those crazy experiments, calculating maths problems, drawing out the countries of East Africa, with their funny shapes and flowing rivers, until I knew them better than the paths that lead to the fields. I used to sit by the pump after my chores, memorizing Shakespeare. All for that pink dress with white flowers. My mother knew it and so she would look in the window in town now and again to make sure that it was still there. When I tired of studying, she would sigh, "That is a pity. That dress would have looked so pretty on you!" And with a smile, I would carry on for a few minutes longer. And so it became a symbol of my progress, my determination, and my father's dream of a better future for me. The dress became a precious hope for us.

'Finally, the results came out. Oh, how proud my mother was! She could not believe that I had come first in my class. Before we went into town, my mother wanted to stop at my father's grave. It was our custom to go there whenever good or ill beset us. When my brother grew yellow and thin from bush fever, we went and prayed for his health; when my sister Chiwoniso got into trouble with the police, we prayed for her safety; and when the crops grew tall and many, we thanked his spirit for his generosity. So, it was natural that now, having achieved one of his dreams, we should return to see him. It was thus that his spirit stayed strong with us. We knelt there and she prayed.

'"Baba va Tinawo, I thank you for keeping your loving eyes on our family. You have not forgotten us; even though you are now in a faraway place, we know you are also near. Today I bring you our daughter, who has brought you much pride. She is going ahead to roads we never crossed. Be with her now as she celebrates her happiness." I glowed and glowed and dreamt of how and when I would wear that dress and how proud he would have been. Yet as we drew near town, I began to grow uneasy. What if the dress had been bought? But to my great relief, there it was, waiting for me – a beautiful little dress, just my size, hanging cool and fresh, in the window. We had never been inside the shop before. We stepped in with determination. A European lady with a sharp nose approached us.

'"I am sorry, we have no work here," she said firmly, waving us away.

'At this my mother reached into her bag and unfolded a fistful of crumpled notes and unknotted a handkerchief of neatly stacked coins. She held them out to the woman and said in her thick but gentle accent, "Please, for my child – the pink dress."

'The woman's nose seemed to grow narrower still, while the tip seemed to glisten like a sword.

'"We don't sell to blacks here. Go to your African shops."

'"But here is the money. The child has worked hard. Please, madam, for the child," she pleaded.

'"Now I've told you, no. You must get out. We have customers to serve." She swerved round and a fellow African who had been lounging at the door was given his terse instructions. "Robert, show them out."

'My mother moved forward again, looking at me, then at her, and pleadingly pushed the money into her hand. "Please, for the child – the dress for her. She wants it so. She has worked you do not know how hard."

'Sword Nose flung the money from her hand and snorted in disgust. "Get out now! It is your stubborn impudence that is ruining our country! Get out! I don't want your dirty kafir money!' she shrieked.

163

'I can still hear the clatter of the coins as they scattered about the room. And I watched with revulsion as my mother bent to her knees, scrambling to collect the fallen coins. I did not move from the spot. I simply looked back and forth between the dress, my mother gathering notes and coins to her bosom, and then at the white woman who sat scowling behind the register. I took it all in, and the scene was like a picture that I took with me that night when, without a word, I crept into the bush and joined the freedom fighters.'

By now, Linda was chopping the onions furiously, so that I could not tell whether the tears that trickled down her face and that she brushed away so impatiently were due to the sadness of the story or the sting of the vegetable.

After a few minutes of silence, Tinawo continued in a stronger voice. 'You know, one night, many months later, when our regiment came into town from the bush to spread the gospel of Chimurenga, we passed by that shop. I saw the dress still hanging there and told the story to one of the comrades. He wanted to smash the store and burn it. But I told him no, that we should save our ammunition for the bigger struggle. I did not want to buy the dress; I wanted to own it and every other thing that was of my sweat. Through the teaching of the struggle, my ambitions had grown beyond the little outfit to encompass the nation. That became my obsession, that became the true sign of my progress, my father's dreams. And *that* I would not allow anyone to deny me. I could not *buy* freedom – I knew that, even at fifteen – but I knew that I could fight for it. I realized that once we had the land, the rest would come with it, for it was from the red earth of the veld that the richness and beauty of Zimbabwe grew. If we gathered the soil

164

to us, if we grew the cotton and spun the cloth, if we coiled the thread and cut the pattern, if we sewed the prints and owned the shop, then never again would we have to beg.'

Linda continued to chop up the vegetables, her eyes swollen and red. We worked in silence now. All that cut the quiet dusk was the crunch of the knife through the raw onions and tomatoes, the hiss of the boiling water and the bubbling of the *sadza* at the fire a few feet away. The girls had disappeared off the winding road, taking their gaiety and laughter and so leaving us to our sombre reflections. I stole glances at my two companions. Neither one of them had the look designated for a *mjiba*.

That was the colloquial term the village folk applied to the young women of the Revolution. They were women of a new generation who wore trousers like men and could aim just as steady. They were women who killed. They were fit and strong, running through the bush brandishing AK47s and machine guns. These were women who crept into the village in the wee hours and sat by the fireside along with the male comrades, their firearms resting beside them, leading us in singing revolutionary songs. On their backs they carried not runny-nosed babies but the hope of a different generation in the form of runs of ammunition, maps, codes and supplies to fuel the battle that ultimately was to lead us to independence. They were as foreign to our traditional image of women as Eskimos. They were a product of the armed struggle. These women fashioned their own identity. They were feared and admired, for in battle it was rumoured the women could be the fiercest of all. The Rhodesian troops called them the 'bobcats' because the Shona women were as fierce as lions.

I sat next to them, these two girls, now women, now guerrillas, whom I had virtually raised. Yet I did not know them. And there was some boundary that could never be crossed. I could tell that they longed for me to understand that part of them that flourished and moved at night in the bush. But it was that very part that I instinctively shied away from. I could not understand it. We had grown up under the same roof, breathed the same air. Why, Linda and I had come out of the same womb, eaten the same food, and worn the same clothes. yet our instincts were opposite. Mine was to retreat to the safety of the cave and hers was to pounce. Linda would devour her predator before he destroyed her. And yet there they sat, young and fresh-faced, with skin that matches your own, smiling at some whimsical truth within, chopping vegetables in the shade of the avocado tree and the setting of the Chakowa sky. It was extraordinary that I had never really grasped the reality of their perilous underground lives.

'I will never understand how you have managed to go on,' I said. 'One day the people will thank you. I am not so brave as you, little sisters. The bush is not for me. I wage my own insignificant, small struggles from day to day. They mean little to anyone but me, it's true. But my door is always open and my pots are always full for you and your friends if you need anything.'

I gathered the pan of seasoned tripe, and without another word, I left them to put the rest of the meat on the fire near the kitchen and pass the dusk with their stories of struggle. When next you are home, you should ask Auntie Linda about her fighting years. She does not talk much about it now; I am not sure why. But it is all there inside her and I know she would be flattered to have you interested in the revolution. So few of the young people are nowadays. Freedom is something you all take for granted. Yet fifty – no, even twenty years ago – it was a dream we dared not even dream.

X

You have a special gift. It is the gift of the third eye. You can see what others cannot, and this is a power that you must cherish and use wisely. You have the ability to create the world that you wish to live in. Nothing is fixed for you. Knots can be untied, chains can be broken, walls can be smashed and doors can be pushed open. For you, that seems obvious. But we had a cousin in our family who married an absolutely wretched drunkard. He beat her terribly every day for the most trifling domestic matters – if his shirt was not ironed properly, if his dinner was undercooked – and it particularly enraged him if she went out with her group of friends, which he eventually banned from the house altogether. Each time they had a row, she fled to our home, sobbing, her face disfigured and oozing blood from some new cut that he had given her. We were always scuttled out of sight as children, but as I grew older, my mother recruited me to assist her, as Linda was still too young. We would fill the large tin bath with steaming hot water, with a few sprigs of herbs that my mother put in to soothe her, in the outhouse, where the shower is now. I washed her very gently from head to toe and watched as the clear water grew pink, then strawberry, then deep red like a tomato. Afterwards we would put cool creams on her bruises and we sheltered her for the night. But to my constant astonishment, the very next morning at sunrise he would come for her. He cooed promises and drew a weary smile from her swollen lips. Sometimes he would even bring flowers. My mother and I would stand on the veranda steps and watch in disbelief as they walked off side by side to their home.

One night when Linda was now fifteen and I was eighteen, we heard a frantic knocking coming from outside Mbuya's window. Both Mbuya and Sekuru had left that morning for Gwelo to visit an ailing aunt. The three boys who worked for us had finished their chores and were off at the shops drinking and playing cards. Linda was terrified. I crept along the dark passage and as I neared Mbuya's bedroom, I heard sobbing and a scratching at the window.

'Ambuya, I beg you, please open the door for me. Please. It is I, Rudo.'

I recognized my cousin's whimper even before she said her name.

'Linda, quickly – go and light some candles, put more wood in the stove, and set some water to boil – it is Sisi Rudo,' I shouted, as I rushed to release the latch on the front door. We did the best that we could to scrub off the caked blood, cool the sore bruises and soothe her. But there was a detached ritualistic precision to our work. Even though she would sob all night, so that in the morning the pillow was soaked through and through and had to be put out to dry, I knew that no matter how high and deep her wails, at daybreak, just as we were finishing our morning tea on the veranda, he would appear and off she would go.

After they had left, I did not know what to say to Linda, as it was the first time that she had been involved and I feared it had been too much for her. It was unlike her to be so silent. I turned to her as we lost sight of them around a corner.

'You were very tough, Linda. You really helped me. I am so used to Mai being here when she comes.'

Linda shrugged her shoulders. 'You know, Sisi Shiri, the blood and the cuts and scars did not bother me as much as her battered spirit.'

'Oh, yes,' I agreed compassionately, 'it is dreadful to hear her cry.'

'No, Sisi Shiri, it is not even the crying. I mean she has been coming here regularly for over five years – she is more regular than the curse. It is ridiculous. If she is so unhappy, why doesn't she just pack her bags and leave him? They do not even have children. She is stupid! Next time I will not wash her. She must decide what she wants. This is not a hotel!'

'Linda!' I could not believe her callousness.

'It's true. She is a grown woman. She can decide how to live her life. It is disgraceful, Sisi Shiri, to allow another person to make you their slave. It is against all that we are as people. She has made herself no better than a dog or a baboon.'

I could see that Linda was really infuriated. I had thought that her silence was sadness. But instead, I understood now that Linda found it incomprehensible and unforgivable that one could be so passive in life. It was almost like a personal affront to her dignity as an African woman and a human being. Come to think of it, I guess Linda was a freedom fighter long before the armed struggle reached our village. In many ways she was right. I had watched my mother try to coax Rudo for years to leave her worthless husband. But she absolutely refused. She said that he was the husband whom God had chosen for her and under His eyes she had vowed to love him for better or for worse. This was her fate, she argued. There was nothing to be done but to cheerfully bear the lot that God had apportioned her. I explained this to Linda, who became even more inflamed.

'Rubbish! That is exactly the spirit of a servant! That is what these missionary churches do for our people! I will bet that every Sunday she gets on her knees in her best starched dress and wails to Reverend Chigare and he tells her to be a good and dutiful wife and things will be better. Yes, I am sure he even tells her not to do anything to upset him so that he won't hit her.' She made a low, snickering sound of disgust.

'Linda, you know that Reverend Chigare is a good man!' I said remonstratively.

'Ayee! You know, Sisi Shiri, what I hate about our churches – they teach people that they cannot do anything to change their lives. All you can do is pray and leave your affairs in the hands of God. As far as I am concerned God helps those who help themselves. The meek may inherit the earth but the rest of us are going to heaven! I mean, honestly. Sisi Rudo can get up and leave that beast. Instead she fixes herself up every Sunday to pray for strength to endure his blows. Then she comes here every month to snivel all night and get a clean bath.'

'Linda! That is no way to talk about the Church or your cousin. Honestly, have you no heart? That is enough. Take the tea things to the boys to wash up.'

This was her parting shot as she disappeared into the shadows of the narrow corridor: 'Yes, thank God, I still have heart. It is Sisi Rudo who has lost hers. She has given up hope and become helpless. She is a disgrace to all women. You wait and see, Sisi Shiri, never will I let life throw me here and there like some dead leaf in a storm. Never, ever. And let any man dare to hit me! Heh!'

At the time I was appalled at her coldness and I could not understand why she took the matter so personally. I later discovered that this was part of the revolutionary mind-set. Self-determination was the cornerstone of their philosophy. Linda had started rebelling against the status quo as a child. She saw alternatives where we did not. She dared to dream a world that bore no relation to the present. She saw Zimbabwe before it existed.

I discovered a similar capacity in your father years later. It was soon after we were married and he was constantly seeing domestics who had been thrown out of their jobs for no reason, families who had lost all their possessions in the war and had no insurance or had been evicted from their homes by soldiers. One night, he described to me the plight of one of his clients who had just been fired from his job and then subsequently evicted from his home with his family of five. Your father came home from a late night with them thoroughly disheartened, which was rare for him. He had seen countless times the very underbelly of human nature as it slithers to bite and poison the lives and minds of others. Yet throughout it all, he had borne a spirited optimism. But that evening, I remember him shaking his head wearily.

'Amai Zenzele, do you believe in fate?' he asked as I was clearing the table.

'Yes, I do. I believe that we cannot change the events of our lives, that they have already been laid out for us.' It was perhaps the only time that I saw him truly disappointed in me. He looked very tired and a grey sadness made his face look old and heavy.

'But how came you to believe this, Shiri?' he asked wearily.

'I don't know. It is just that you can try and try to keep something or possess something of your own, but if it is not God's will, it will be taken from you. You can pray, you can clutch, you can dream, hope, and watch, but at some moment when you are least expecting it, some greater force will make a fool of you and take what it will. Ultimately, the universe is predetermined: we are simply the little scattered jigsaw pieces of a prearranged picture that has long been created and assembled by the gods.' As I finished clearing the dishes, I accidently dropped a knife as I reached out to collect his plate.

'Shiri, what is the matter? Your hands are trembling like mad. Here, give me those plates.' He reached out but it was too late; the plates fell to the floor with a crash that brought the maid rushing out. Your father reached out to take my hands in his, but I pulled back.

'It is nothing,' I said. 'It is simply that you reminded me of something I thought was buried long ago. Really, I am all right. Let Sisi clear up and make coffee for us in the study.' He looked at me now with new intensity and curiosity. I only managed to distract him by steering him out of the dining room, clasping my hands in a tight interlock behind my back, and asking with fervent but fake interest, 'Why did you ask me if I believed in fate?'

He sat down and looked absorbed in thought.

'Lately, I have become greatly discouraged by the beaten spirits of the majority of most of my clients. They come to me with their problems and I try to help them. But it is a tremendous task because they are so resigned and fearful. They want things to change, yet they do not want to be the pioneers of change. In fact, I am not even sure it is that they do not *want* to be, but they do not *believe* that they have the power to affect the events that assail them. So many of them have been thoroughly indoctrinated by these bloody missionaries!'

I had long given up defending the Church but I did feel compelled to make him understand. 'Baba va Zenzele, do not be too harsh on them: they do not have the spirit and confidence that comes so easily to your nature. It is not that one is born helpless. It is just that after years of fighting impossible battles, gaining nothing but weariness and impoverishment, you learn your limits and live as best you can given the dark realities of existence.'

'But, Shiri, this is cowardice! There are things that we can change. Too many people give up too soon; they do not fight for what is truly theirs. The Government, Church and television keep the average man so mired in petty concerns that he can no longer discern which battles are worth fighting for. For that matter, even if he had a consciousness, he would be too exhausted to face a struggle. Look at this country! Our people scramble here and there cleaning, polishing and ploughing for the rich white man. They smile all day in the heat, raping the land of their fathers for less than minimum wage so that foreigners may reap the profits. It is pitiful. The tragedy is that the irony and the absurdity of their circumstance elude them entirely. They should be fighting for this land; it is theirs. The evicted do not know housing laws, the maimed are ignorant of disability laws, the blind cannot read the rights of the handicapped, the battered wife has no idea of her rights, and so on. Yet they can each of them quote all the platitudes. "Blessed are the meek, for they shall inherit the earth," they say with a sigh. It is extraordinary how ignorance and resignation have completely disarmed our people.' He shook his head slowly from side to side. He was so sullen, and all the more because he perceived me as being from the other world – that of the disempowered. I often wondered how we had come to be one when we had such disparate maps of the world. He stood at the hilltop, triumphant in his struggles. I, on the other hand, roamed the cool, sheltered valleys below. But somehow we had found a common stream, a shared pasture where we could meet.

Unlike your father, I had long ago ceased to dream. For a brief time in my youth, I had believed that I could fight for what was mine. But how does one fight death? It is the ultimate humbler. At the moment you face death, you finally understand that all our pretence of directing and controlling our lives is futile. God takes whomever he pleases, whenever he pleases, almost as a mocking reminder of our helplessness. Yet over the years, my cynicism has been mitigated as I watch with awe as your father has achieved what others would not dare. I have seen him, through the power of his words, give the battered woman her rights, the homeless a roof, the unemployed a job. Through his own firm, confident voice he has made strikers heard, given women the right to vote, and offered children protection from abuse and ignorance. He dares to challenge reality because for him the present construct is simply the realization of someone else's vision. Your father has the confidence to believe that his vision is brighter and more just than the one in which we toil. And so he rises at dawn each day to go to farms, factories and mines to spread his version of reality. Those who were silent begin to sing songs of freedom. Those who used to sit at the bar drowning their powerlessness in a long draught of local brew have taken to pounding the streets, marching for their rights. Every day, he seems to cast his own fate aside and walk a fresh path, so confounding the gods that they have abandoned him to his own will. So that each day he brings his vision one step further to truth. Thus I have come to believe that there are a chosen few: your father, my sister Linda, my cousin Tinawo and yourself who are blessed with the gift of the third eye – the vision that empowers, that makes you bold to laugh in the face of Fate's stern, set, furious glare, to ignore the path that she has pointed out for you and opt for some other, grassier path to tread. It is for you to sway the course of destiny, it is your words that will write the text of a new chapter of African history. In that version there will be no place for victims, only leaders. There is a tremendous responsibility that comes with this vision of which the rest of us are blissfully ignorant. Once you see the alternatives and are convinced of their merit, you will be obliged like some new religious zealot to spread it, to convert others, and never to tire of the mission.

I have often thought about my cousin Rudo. She subsequently had two miscarriages because of her husband's beatings. Her only child, a son, Nyaradzo, was born deaf and blind. Perhaps it was God's mercy that sheltered him from the screams of his mother and the brutal sight of her abuse and degradation. To this day, she lives with her husband in Chakowa. I wonder how and when she, too, ceased to dream. When and why did she cease to ask, What if? What died in her? What led her to this profound despair that permits her to live apathetically in a marriage of such barbarous injustice?

Who muted that little internal voice that should never fail to wonder, 'Is this all there is?' Who trampled that part of her that should ask, 'Dear God, can this truly be my lot?'

XI

I wonder too about God. Here I can offer you no guidance. It has taken over a decade for me to reconcile myself with my God. I know that there is good and that she has a twin sister – evil – and I have met them both. They are simply two sides of a coin. If one toss settles here, there is joy, but should the throw land on the other side there is anguish. I have seen so many of our people, myself included, settle for the unbearable present in the hope of what is to come. That is what the Africans of America were told to do, too. Hush, with a load of cotton on your back like a mule, say nothing of the stinging cotton as it pricks your fingers while you, stooped low, are ordered to pick. Faster! Faster! They were told not to groan in the scorching heat at work, never to complain of the pains from sleeping on the hard, cold floor, never mind the hovel that you call home and the misery that you call life. This, too, shall pass. Pray to God and you shall be rewarded, not here on earth, but in heaven. Of all God's people, our race is the one that has most consistently forsaken this life and kept its hopes steadfast on the world to come. But I always wondered, what if that world never comes?

It can be terribly difficult at times to be at peace within. I wanted a smooth life. But I have learned that the furrows and ridges of inconsistency and pain are the very contours that give life a meaningful form. I can rage at the heavens for taking away my sculptor, but I must simultaneously thank them for the blessed gift that is you. Actually, the most moving religious experience I had was with you. You were only six years old then. You had insisted on accompanying me to drop off your Uncle Farai, who was only fourteen himself, back at his boarding school, Cyrene Mission, after a long weekend at our home. Having seen him settled in comfortably and having given him a little pocket money, you and I wandered hand in hand to the historic chapel, which I had never visited. You ran ahead, giggling, and suddenly stopped before the murals that decorate the chapel.

'Mama, look! Look at the angels!'

I stopped in my tracks too. I had been to thousands of glorious cathedrals and churches abroad with spiralling towers and gothic proportions, yet none struck me as beautiful as this humble little chapel. Never in my life had I seen black angels. I paced slowly around the church, following the flight of each little black cherub. One sat cross-legged atop a fluffy white cloud, praying with a serene expression of complete devotion. Her shiny gold wings enclosed her and her golden halo hung above her, emitting a radiance that caught the glow of her deep brown cheeks and made her face shine. Another laughed in joy at the adulation of the saints next to her, while a pair just above her puffed their cheeks and spread their wings wide as they blew their trumpets to announce the coming of Christ.

'Mama, that one looks like Joy! Look. This one looks

like me! Look at her hair, Mama, even her eyes. I could be an angel too, Mama. Hoorah! I never knew!'

You were dancing all around the building now, laughing and giggling, darting here and there, puffing out your cheeks pretending to be blowing on a trumpet.

'Look, I am an angel, Mama. See! Parrrum, parrrum!' You blew out your cheeks and flapped your arms while skipping around the chapel. I looked away so that you wouldn't see the tears in my eyes. Inside, too, was full of Africans: John the Baptist, standing dark and strong in the river, blessing and preaching to the masses. Moses with his long white beard looked a little like Babamukuru with his wide nose flaring, and the curls of his Afro looked as if they had a life of their own as he put forward God's commandments. Then there was the scene that caused me to sit in the nearest pew and gaze in wonder. There was Jesus Christ himself, with wavy black hair, skin of brown earth, and deep clay eyes that looked down at me with such a pitying smile. They seemed to say, 'Where have you been? I have been here all this time waiting for you.' It was the first time that I had looked at an icon and felt that he could see me as I truly was. Of course it was only an idol. But the impact of having oneself reflected there was mesmerizing. There was God himself in my own image and not the image of my oppressors. I dropped to my knees. Here was the God I had been searching for. Not the Teutonic God that I had been told to worship for all these years at missionary schools. Who had deprived me of this vision? This God knew me. His cross was my cross; his people were my people. Mary, Joseph, Peter, Mark and John – all black like me!

'Mama, look at Jesus. He looks like Baba when he smiles!'

'Zenzele, shoosh!' I hissed, overwhelmed.

'But Mama, this is not a cinema. Why do I have to whisper?'

I gave no response. How could I, when inside me my head was exploding with new images and new faith. I could not believe that I had almost deprived you of an identification with Christianity for all these years. Worst of all, I had deprived myself. I resumed going to church that year. I left the Methodist church in town and took trips to Cyrene to see my God whenever I could get away. I even joined the Orthodox Ethiopian Church, where all the images were of our likeness and the customs were rooted in our culture.

That evening you crawled into our bedroom.

'Zenzele, what are you doing? You should be asleep!' your father scolded.

'Look, Baba!' you said in the sweetest voice, standing up on our bed, not unaware of your charm and twirling about so that the white sheet you had wrapped around you flowed like a cape. 'Don't be afraid. I am an angel – just like the ones at church today. Isn't that so, Mama?'

And indeed you did resemble exactly one of those little brown cherubim, except your eyes were sparkling, full of mischievous life. Even then your eyes were of such a depth that they startled one to look too long there. I trembled as I held you in my arms. In the middle of the night I smiled as I kissed an angel slumbering in a little heap between us. From that day forward, all our Christmas angels had brown skin and black hair.

The strength of your conviction was a source of inspiration itself. I remember an incident just before Christmas. You were eight and you had Mary

Ringweitter over to colour and play. Not a half hour after her arrival you came charging into the kitchen, furiously shaking a drawing in front of me.

'Look, Mama, she coloured the angels wrong!'

'Did not!' pouted your friend, brushing away her tears.

'Did so! Angels are brown! You can't do any more unless you do it right!' You snatched the yellow and peach crayons from her hand.

'Zenzele!' I reprimanded.

'She says there is no such thing as black angels, Mama. That's a lie! Tell her about the church!' you said, looking at me with such earnest conviction, it paled the devotion of the saints and angels at the mission.

And so it came to be that every so often we packed a car full of disbelieving schoolmates, and soon their parents too, and drove off to Cyrene Mission. And you always emerged dancing about the murals to counter their surprised expressions with a smug, 'See. I told you so!'

I marvelled at those little mustard-seed-sized eyes that believed so strongly. I wondered how I might have come to resolve the issue of God in my life if I had believed at the outset that I was truly created in His image and not some dubious offshoot of a forgotten tribe; if I had truly believed that Christianity was my religion rather than some pacifying myth dreamed up by the missionaries, the plantation managers, the giant soft-drink manufacturers, the rich diamond multi-nationals and the big explorers whose chief interest was to keep our hands industrious (and so profitable) in this life but our minds placid and fixed on the world to come. But you and your father converted me to a real belief. Not in an all-powerful, omniscient and benign

God but of the empiric, contradictory, jealous and spontaneous one who preferred the company of prostitutes and lepers to hypocrites; the one who lied to Adam and Eve about the fruit of knowledge and then banished them from the Garden of Eden; the one who could wipe out an entire civilization in a rage, who could make a promise and keep it or sit passively and watch while the devil tested his most faithful believers with all manner of plague and misfortune. It is the God who returns to the Garden of Eden, surprised, and thus not all-knowing, that Adam and Eve had disobeyed him. The one, too, who could create for us a paradise like Eden, he who could love so deeply and counsel so wisely. Him, the one with the deep brown eyes and curly Afro is the one I believe in now. I no longer see the world as ready-made, requiring only that we occupy our own little spot and do unto others as we would have them do unto us, as they taught me at the Sunday School in Chakowa Mission. Like your father, I am coming to understand that this world is as yet unfinished. There is no Eden here save the one we create for one another. Our mission is to complete and preserve the work that was started. And that is why we are created in God's image.

Oh dear! It is late now! Samuel has already started to rake away the dead leaves and clear the lawn. I can hear Joy crying, up in the nursery, refusing her morning bath as usual, and poor Sisi trying to coax her. The kitchen will be invaded soon. Here is your father already approaching in search of coffee, a quaint Americanism he picked up in his university days there. I must dash. You are not to worry about me. The doctors have no diagnosis for these pains and this sapping of my strength. And as I have told your father so many times, no news is good news, as they say! I shall have to continue this letter later, as I am off to the country.

XII

Chakowa, Zimbabwe

I am at Chakowa, sitting in my father's sagging old chair, looking out beyond the valley to the setting of the sun. I have come here to be alone and yet embraced. This old house is so cluttered with memories that as I wander through the corridors, I bump and stumble upon the echoes and visions of times past. Last night as I lay reading by candlelight, I swear I heard the low rumble of my father's deep bass humming 'Ne rimwe Zuva'. Oh, how he loved that song. After he died, I often used to sing it to myself on lonely nights. I wonder if it is really true, as we believe, that we shall all meet again. But where? And in what form? Will you be my daughter in the life to come, or will we be sisters of a common spirit? What happens to our love when we die? I wonder. Do we take it with us? Or does it mould and decay like the flesh? What became of my mother's faith? Did my father's firm, quiet wisdom evaporate with his last breath? It cannot be so, for what use then is this life? No, I believe, as our ancestors believed, that we pass on gifts to one another at the time of death. Just as we distribute the garments of the deceased to family and close friends, so, too, the dead will bestow their spirit among those they love. I remember how after my father died my mother became stronger yet gentler. She seemed to merge his best traits to temper her own. I believe that they were bound so closely in life that they could not part at death, and so their wedded spirit lived on in her. And now they lie side by side, united once again, in the shade of the orange and mango trees that line the stream flowing below our family plot.

Before she passed from this life to join him, my mother used to visit my father's grave every day at dawn, even after the arthritis that burned her joints had knotted her hands and bowed her knees. She awoke before the sun pierced the darkness. We could hear her kettle hiss at the stove and the swish and splash of the water as she filled her bath. Those morning sounds served as our alarm clock, that and our macho rooster, who, catching the slightest hint of light, would strut to the veranda and, perching himself on the ledge, facing the sun, bellow a throaty, uneven cry that heralded the beginning of another day's work. I did not rise right away. Nor did it occur to any of us to go along with her. I only accompanied her on those trips on Sundays and special occasions. But I watched her from our window as she tucked her cloak tightly to her to keep out the morning chill, and set off into the darkness. For many minutes, I would hear the uneven rhythm of her cane as she passed the outhouses, then mounted the dirt path that led past Amai Byron's bungalow and down past the shops to the prickly path that led to our family graveyard. And well I knew the ritual that she would engage in once she arrived there, for we repeated it each week. As she would pass the small mounds of earth that marked the resting places of our great-grandparents, she would curtsey and beg leave to pass, giving due respect to her elders. Then, upon entering 'the modern wing' as you call it, where the last generation are buried and their graves are marked with ornate stones and engravings, she always said a little prayer beside the tan square slab that marks the tomb of my aunt, Tete Mercy, who had been like a sister to her but had died a tragic death in a bus accident many years before. Then she would advance more quickly in the eager but restrained anticipation of visiting a friend. And so indeed she was. She always said, 'Excuse me, Baba va Shiri. It is I, Mai va Shiri. I have come to visit.' And so she daily re-established their connection, their bond. He was still the father and she was the mother. She would kneel and say a prayer, and then, crossing herself, she sat at the edge of the marble slab that formed the foundation of his tombstone, turning her back to the others and facing the stream. Then she would slowly and quietly bare her soul. Not in any dramatic or emotional manner, but in her even, matter-of-fact style, she simply told him what had happened the day before and what she planned for the day ahead. She always mentioned us, where we were, what our grades were at school, how we behaved ourselves, who we played with and how big we were. She would even chuckle about funny things she had heard (she always saved the village gossip for last) and things we had done. From the path she looked quite mad, sitting at the edge of a tombstone talking and shaking her head with an occasional chuckle. Initially, I was afraid that she had become senile, but her mind at home, in the fields and at church was as sharp as ever. Amai Byron told me that when a man and woman had become one they could speak to each other in ways that others could not understand. She told me that love transcended everything. I remember how surprised I was, for it had never occurred to me that my parents loved each other. Yet they were as one, and gentle to each other in all things.

Sekuru Dumisani had told Linda, Farai, Lucy, a distant cousin, and me, when we were girls, the story of two lovers who had purportedly lived in our village years ago, and it reminded me of the bond my parents had even after death. Dikani and Rudo were young and passionately in love, but their union was vehemently opposed by their parents. They always met clandestinely but eventually were discovered and once again separated and forbidden to see each other. Nevertheless their passion was so strong that they managed somehow to meet and communicate. As the years passed, the burden of inventing new ways of meeting and finding messengers and accomplices they could trust grew too heavy as one after another of their schemes was discovered by their parents. In desperation they visited a *n'anga*, a spiritualist, who gave them a potion that would put them to sleep forever without pain. And so they donned their best clothing and she borrowed a traditional wedding dress. In the middle of the night, they stole away. They chose the clearing near the avocado orchards of the Matiziva plot. They clasped each other tightly by one hand and, with their other, took the potion. And that is how they were found the next morning, like bride and groom, with their hands entwined and wearing triumphant but cool, distant smiles – quite dead. The parents were so disgusted at their children's betrayal that they buried them, each in their separate family plot, without any ceremony and without speaking to one another. For years, the families were haunted by restless spirits. There were noises in the night; misfortune befell them; their crops failed year after year; strange and incurable illnesses weakened the young and plagued the elderly. Finally, they consulted a priestess, who instructed them that in order to appease the ancestors for severing the budding roots of true love, they had to rebury their children in the proper fashion and make peace with one another. The families came together for the first time and agreed to be reconciled, and so ended their ancient feuding. When they set to the task of reburial, they discovered to their great horror that the coffin of Dikani was empty. Amai Byron, who claims to have seen it, swears that the inside was as pristine as a new coffin. There was not a hair or chip of bone, just a gleaming, empty, satin-lined coffin. The next day, they dug up Rudo's grave. Inside were two ghostly and emaciated cadavers lying side by side, their bony hands entwined, with strands of te-thered, decayed flesh here and there. The poor *n'anga*, with the aid of two other priestesses, had to rebury them in a single large coffin, side by side, as the families were overcome with terror. This time they were laid to rest with a traditional ceremony in the bush at the spot that they had chosen to meet and join hands years earlier. The families performed every traditional rite before and after the funeral that the *n'angas* could think of: in all, twenty goats and ten cows were slaughtered, herbs were gathered and concoctions were brewed to appease the spirits. It is said that in that spot there grows a tree with two trunks that twist around and around each other and whose branches are interlocked. It has the sweetest fruit and the most beautiful orange and fuchsia blooms that are fragrant all year long. But if you pick a fruit from one side, one on the exact opposite side will drop to the ground. It is a tree of perfect symmetry, balance and union. Only fearless lovers go to the spot.

There is, for all of its beauty, something frightening there.

Anyway, that is supposedly why it is said that within our clan the spirit of love is stronger than the laws of physics. And so it seemed natural after a time to see my mother from the road, sitting among scattered, ominous mounds of earth, crooked wooden crosses and carved tombstones, calm and peaceful, talking to a slab of mute marble. The myths of our culture, after all, say that our love stays with us in life and in the unknown hereafter. It transcends all things.

In times of trouble, I have often come to Chakowa, the home of my ancestors, to seek the peace that their spirit brings. This morning, I awoke very early, and after a cup of tea, stumbled out into the semidarkness to the family graveyard. From the road I must have looked as my mother did all those years ago as I sat facing my parents' tombstones, laid side by side, and told them of this illness, this thing inside me that they call a growth, as if it were something beautiful and creative. Instead it is eating at me, taking away my strength. I told them of your progress in America and how proud we are that you have already started to organize among the African students. I told them how your father still works too hard, that even though the armed struggle of independence is long over, there is never a want of underprivileged and forgotten people. I unburdened all this and walked slowly back along the dusty path. I felt lighter, as if I had indeed sat with my father and told him my joys and troubles. I heard no voices, but the answers were in the lightness of my heart and the clarity of my thoughts, as if spirit had answered spirit in a form that eluded the mortal tongue. There must be generations of spirits here, but I am not afraid. No, I feel stronger just being here. As I crossed over the Umvumvumvu River, I thought to myself that we are all bridges. We form a link between the past and the future. Perhaps one day, you, too, will come here and when the world has overcome you with its madness you will awake at dawn, slip on a veil of black lace and sit by my tombside and talk. You must not feel foolish, for I shall be sure to answer you in whatever way one touches another after death. But I have not come to the home of my birth to be morbid but rather to seek peace and reflect.

I have come, you see, to a strange fork in the road. It is so very odd to look back and see the path that I have trodden, now overgrown and distant, and wonder, What if? What if I had taken the road of my sister and cousins and darted into the bush to join the armed struggle? What if, like Mukoma Byron, I had flown off to London? Was this, then, my destiny? Or perhaps somewhere back there, in the dense thicket of re-trospection, I wandered astray. But that is behind me. I stand at the crossroads of life, with what could have been behind and what must be ahead. It is admittedly an awkward place to be. So much has changed, the scenes of a new culture, the mixing of races that was pro-hibited in my day, the opening of an entire nation to our people. But oddly, too, there coexists the timeless poverty of the villages, the fear, the old prejudices, the familiar injustices and the eternal existence of evil. These things have not changed; my parents saw these before me and you shall observe them after me. It is true that I have not fought. My name shall never appear on the roster of famous battles. To be sure, no great landscape or colossal sculpture or impassioned poem shall bear my signature. I shall not be flying to Rome or

London or Oslo for any awards. It is true that I have had no great visions. But I have loved, and surely this is enough. It is to have tasted from the cup of milk and honey. And what need do I have of shiny badges for bravery? Courage is, after all, to take great risks – and in loving, I have known the pain of risk and loss.

And, there is you. Should anyone ask what my contribution is to this world, I can only say that my conscience rests joyously with the knowledge that I had a hand in bringing you into it. And what is time but a measure of change? When the sun rises, it is day, and when it rolls away, it is night. Summer is simply winter with warmth and colour. And so from birth to death is measured a lifetime. I have seen the seasons come and go and I feel as if I have lived several lifetimes, for I have seen the order of things turn and spin and turn again. What was white became black; what was evil became good. It is this that ultimately gives me peace. For I have lived many lives through the stories of my ancestors and the tales of those whom I have loved. This I have to treasure for eternity. I shall sing my stories in the morning with the birds and in the gales of the rains, with the howling winds and crackling thunder. If you listen deep within, you will hear the echo of this letter no matter where your heart leads you.

It is a pity that I have not more to leave you than words. But what is a life, after all, but a story, some fiction and some truth? In the end, there are words. They are the very manifestations of our immortality. Your own life is a story yet to be told, and wisdom, when it comes, is simply to understand at last the beginning of the word and the story of our birth, death and rebirth.

How shall I say good-bye to you, Zenzele? You, you

my little earthquake. Who will rock my world now that you are so far away? You have given me such joy. I have so much more to tell you, but it will have to wait for next time because my hand aches. Until we meet again, be it on earth or beyond, go well, Zenzele. Be strong.

Your friend,
Mama